My Top Score Activity Book

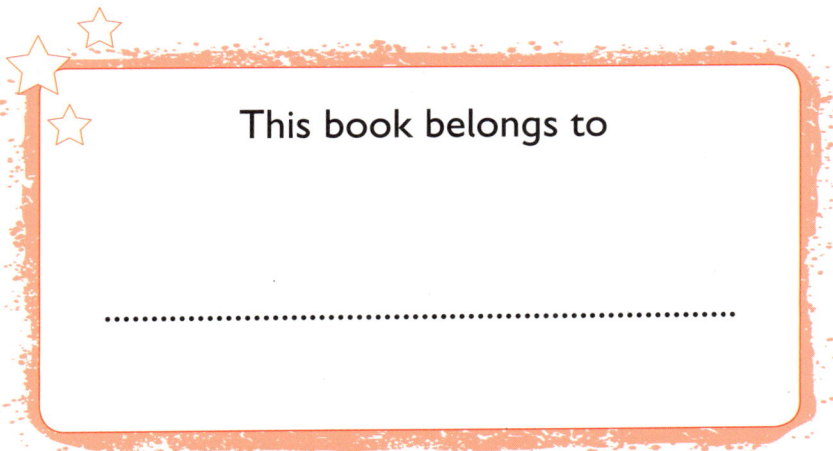

This book belongs to

....

Lyn Jones

Contents

Clever Crocodiles 4
The Taj Mahal 6
Egyptian Gods and Goddesses .. 8
Climates and Plants 10
Coral Reefs 12
Mount Vesuvius 14
Wildlife with Wings 16
High Peaks 18
Working in Ancient Times 20
Harsh Places 22
Space and the Solar System 24
Moonwalk 26
Tails Old and New 28
The Roller Coaster 30
Making a Mummy 32
Sneaky Spiders 34
Making the Moon 36

No More 38
Dino Babies 40
Inventions at Home 42
Bright Colours 44
Reef Hunters 46
Tornado! 48
All about Helicopters 50
St Basil's Cathedral 52
School in Ancient Times 54
Long Horns 56
The Sun 58
Giant Plant-eater 60
The Roman Senate 62
The *Titanic* 64
The Sinking of the *Titanic* 66
Hot-air Balloons 68
Danger Looms 70

Everyday Life in Pompeii............72	Up High............................... 106
Telling Time 74	Travelling Overland.................. 108
Military Aircraft 76	Mighty Meat-eater 110
Safe Homes 78	Mummy Cases.......................... 112
Star Gazing 80	Cold Extremes 114
Dangerous Icebergs................... 82	Healthy and Fit in Ancient Greece 116
Sydney Opera House 84	
At Home in Ancient Greece...... 86	Bicycles and Tyres 118
Leafy Seadragons 88	Strong Swimmers...................... 120
Sea and Wind Power.................. 90	Forbidden City 122
Moon Base 92	Comets in Orbit........................ 124
The Dinosaur Disappears 94	Cleaner Shrimps 126
Reefs and People 96	A Pharaoh's Funeral 128
Warning Signs of a Volcano......98	Long and Sticky........................ 130
Hunters and Fishers 100	
Chapters of History................... 102	Join the Dots 132
Going to the Moon 104	Answers 134

Clever Crocodiles

Let's learn about crocodiles. Complete the fun activities when you have finished reading the story. They will help you discover more about the world around you.

Crocodiles do not have to work hard to find food. They lie still, floating in the water until an animal comes near. Then they spring suddenly into action. They grab their victim in strong jaws. Crocodiles can look like logs in the water. They keep most of their body under the water. Their eyes and nostrils stay above the water. Crocodiles are some of the oldest living reptiles on Earth.

1. Read the story carefully and then read these sentences. Are they True (T) or False (F), or is there Not Enough Information (NEI) for you to decide?
   Colour in the star next to the correct answer.

   (a) Crocodiles look like floating logs. ☆ T ☆ F ☆ NEI
   (b) Crocodiles poison their victims. ☆ T ☆ F ☆ NEI
   (c) Dinosaurs are older than crocodiles. ☆ T ☆ F ☆ NEI
   (d) Crocodiles do not eat pelicans. ☆ T ☆ F ☆ NEI
   (e) Crocodiles breathe through the nostrils. ☆ T ☆ F ☆ NEI

2. Which words in the story mean the same as these words? Circle the correct answers.

(a) nostrils

    ears   mouth   nose

(b) jaws

    mouth   eyes   feet

3. Fill in the missing vowels in these sentences.

Vowels: a e i o u

Cr__ cod__ les d__ n__ t have t__ w__ rk h__ rd to f__ nd f__ __ d. Th__ y l__ e st__ ll in th__ w__ t__ r w__ iting unt__ l __ n anim__ l c__ m__ s n__ ar. Then th__ y gr__ b th__ ir v__ ct__ m in th__ ir str__ ng j__ ws.

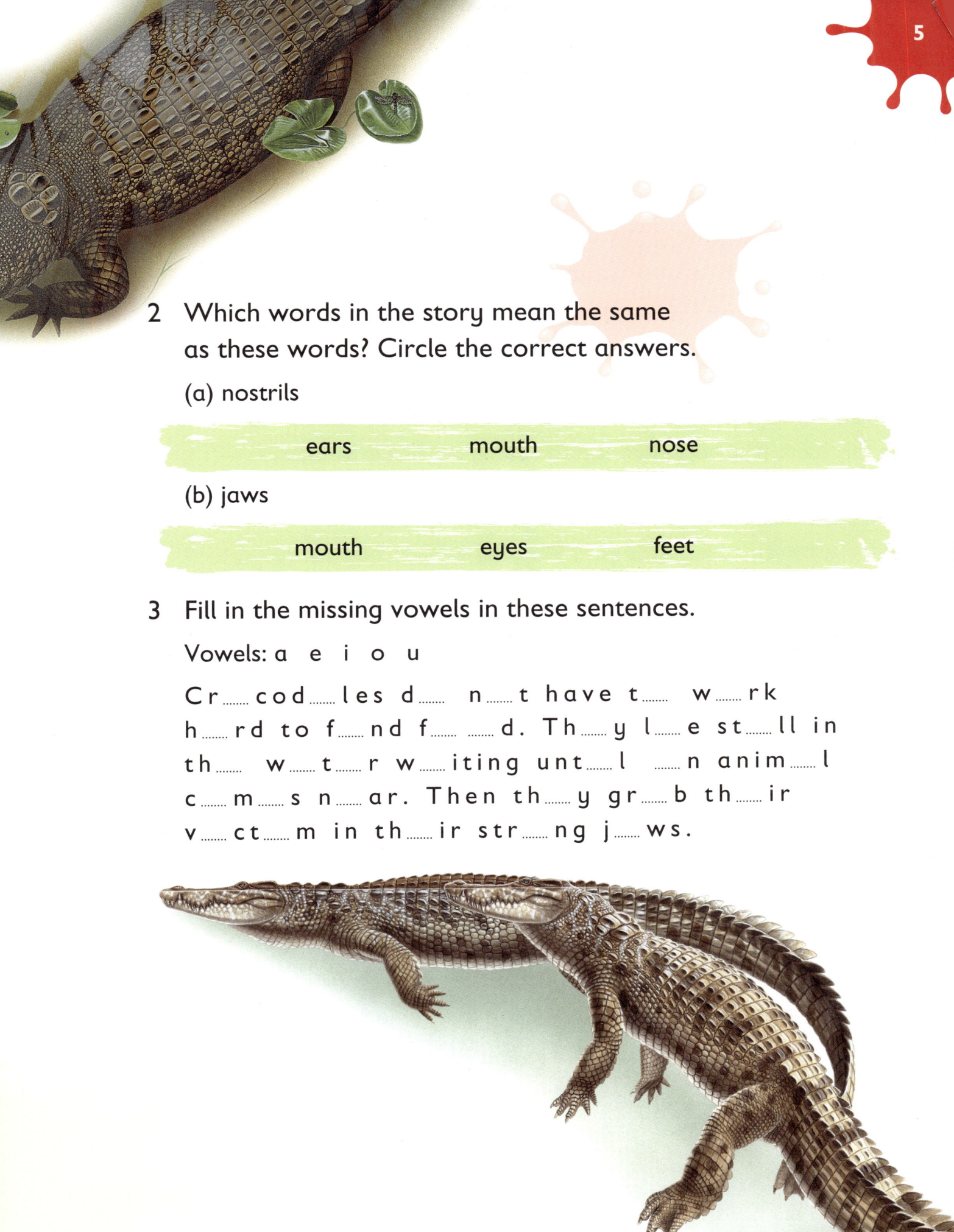

The Taj Mahal

Read this story about a great building called the Taj Mahal. If you find a new word, look at the words around it to help work out the meaning.

Shah Jahan was a ruler in northern India. In 1631 his wife died. To help remember her, he built a magnificent marble tomb called the Taj Mahal. When Shah Jahan died, he was also buried in this tomb. The huge dome on top of the building is 61 metres high. It does not matter from which side you look at it, the Taj Mahal looks the same. The sides are identical.

1 Read the questions. Colour in the star next to the correct answer.

(a) Who was Shah Jahan?
☆ a painter   ☆ a slave   ☆ a ruler

(b) How many people are buried in the Taj Mahal?
☆ one person   ☆ two people   ☆ three people

(c) Where in the world will you see the Taj Mahal?
☆ Shah Jahan   ☆ southern India   ☆ northern India

2 Are these sentences True or False? Write your answers in the spaces below.

(a) The Taj Mahal was built a long time ago.   ....

(b) Each side of the Taj Mahal is different.   ....

(c) Shah Jahan built the Taj Mahal as a burial place.   ....

3   Here's a fun crossword. The answers are words in the story.

   1. burial place
   2. a type of rock
   3. large
   4. same
   5. king

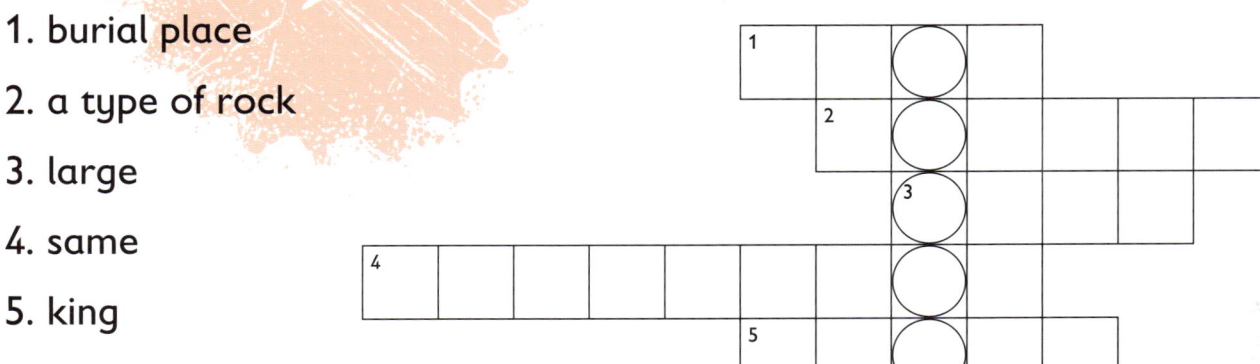

4   The circled letters in the puzzle make up another word from the story. What is it? ....

How many domes are in the picture?

Egyptian Gods and Goddesses

Here is some information about Egyptian gods and goddesses. Read the story. Try to sound out new words. Then enjoy completing the activities.

The ancient Egyptians worshipped many gods and goddesses. They believed that the god Horus was in charge of the land of Egypt. The people also believed that the ruler, or pharaoh, was a god as well. The pharaoh could control the weather and how the crops grew. In this Egyptian wall painting, several gods are shown as human with animal heads. Horus has a falcon's head. Osiris was the god of the dead. If a person had led a good life, their soul could live with Osiris in the Afterlife.

1. Read the story carefully and then read these sentences. Are they True (T) or False (F), or is there Not Enough Information (NEI) for you to decide? Colour in the star next to the correct answer.

   (a) The ancient Egyptians believed in many gods.   ☆ T   ☆ F   ☆ NEI

   (b) Horus was said to be in charge of the land.   ☆ T   ☆ F   ☆ NEI

   (c) The Egyptians gods were cruel.   ☆ T   ☆ F   ☆ NEI

   (d) Some gods had animal heads.   ☆ T   ☆ F   ☆ NEI

   (e) Egyptians believed that the pharaoh was an animal.   ☆ T   ☆ F   ☆ NEI

   (f) Osiris was the god of water.   ☆ T   ☆ F   ☆ NEI

   (g) Horus was a kind god.   ☆ T   ☆ F   ☆ NEI

Anubis   Osiris   Isis   Horus

2 Which god is which? Use the story and the picture to help you answer this question. Colour the stars that fit the description.

	Anubis	Osiris	Isis	Horus
(a) has a white hat	☆	☆	☆	☆
(b) is holding a cross	☆	☆	☆	☆
(c) is holding a spear	☆	☆	☆	☆
(d) controls the land of Egypt	☆	☆	☆	☆
(e) lives in the Afterlife	☆	☆	☆	☆
(f) has a wristband	☆	☆	☆	☆

3 Draw and label your favourite Egyptian god or goddess in the box.

Climates and Plants

Here is some information about how plants depend on the weather and climate. Read the story. Try to sound out new words. Then enjoy completing the activities.

In some places, many plants and trees cover Earth's surface. In other places, only a few types of plants can grow. The kinds of plants that grow in a region depend on the climate. Plants and trees grow easily in warm, wet areas. In deserts few things grow. In cold climates most plants stay close to the ground. In cooler or warmer climates, leafy trees and grasses grow. The tropics are the hottest, wettest parts of Earth's surface.

1 Do these pairs of sentences have the Same (S) meaning or a Different (D) meaning? Colour in the star next to the correct answer.

(a) (i) In some places, many plants and trees cover Earth's surface.

   (ii) Earth's surface is covered by many plants and trees in some places. ☆ S ☆ D

(b) (i) In quite cold places, few types of plants grow well.

   (ii) In cold places, quite a few types of plants grow well. ☆ S ☆ D

2 Match the jigsaw parts to make sentences.
Use different colours to match the sentence parts.

The tropics are	most plants stay	a few plants grow.
In cold climates	a hot, wet	and grasses grow.
In deserts	leafy trees	close to the ground.
In warm climates	grow easily	in warm, wet areas.
Trees and plants	only	part of Earth's surface.

3 Unscramble these letters to make words from the story.

ergion ....

tesmacli ....

esrtsed ....

ucerfsa ....

the tropics

Coral Reefs

What do you know about coral reefs? Read the story and use a dictionary to find the meaning of new words. Try the word puzzles, too.

Corals are very tiny sea creatures. They have a soft body. Corals build a hard shell, or skeleton, around their body. The skeleton is formed from things in seawater. As they grow, corals leave these skeletons behind. The skeletons then build up into a coral reef. A coral reef gives food and shelter for many kinds of sea plants, fish, sponges, shellfish and some sharks.

1 Here's a fun crossword. The answers are words in the story.

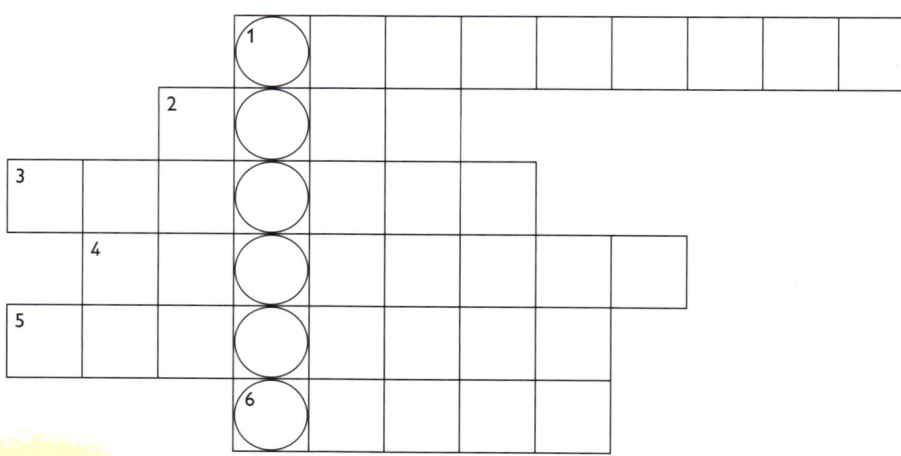

1. animals
2. opposite to hard
3. large, scary fish
4. where corals live
5. bones of the body
6. hard skeleton around coral

2 The circled letters in the puzzle make up a keyword from the story. What is it? ....

3 What are the opposites of these words or phrases? The answers are in the story.

(a) soft ....   (d) takes ....

(b) hard ....   (e) few ....

(c) large ....   (f) take down ....

4 Read the story carefully and then read these sentences. Are they True (T) or False (F), or is there Not Enough Information (NEI) for you to decide?
Colour in the star next to the correct answer.

(a) A coral reef is made up of coral skeletons.   ☆ T   ☆ F   ☆ NEI

(b) Sharks eat coral.   ☆ T   ☆ F   ☆ NEI

(c) Coral is poisonous.   ☆ T   ☆ F   ☆ NEI

(d) Sea sponges find shelter in coral.   ☆ T   ☆ F   ☆ NEI

Can you see six types of fish in this picture?

Mount Vesuvius

Read the story about the lost city of Pompeii. If you find a new word, look at the words around it to help work out the meaning.

Mount Vesuvius is a volcano in Italy. In AD 79, it erupted and buried the city of Pompeii. At that time, the people of Pompeii did not know that Mount Vesuvius was a volcano. It erupted in a huge mushroom-shaped cloud of smoke. Hot rock and ash rained down over the city. People died when buildings collapsed, or from the hot ash and poisonous gas. The world forgot about the city. Many hundreds of years later, Pompeii was rediscovered.

1   Answer these questions about the story.

(a) Where in the world is the lost city of Pompeii?

....

(b) How was the city 'lost' or destroyed?

....

(c) Do you think that the people of Pompeii were foolish to build a city near Mount Vesuvius? Why?

....

2. Think about what happens first, next and last in the story. Number these sentences to show the correct order.

.... Mount Vesuvius erupts.

.... Pompeii is rediscovered.

.... The people of Pompeii do not know that Mount Vesuvius is a volcano.

.... Pompeii is forgotten.

.... Pompeii is buried under hot ash and rock.

3. Look at the picture. Choose the best phrase to finish each sentence.

> hot rocks are falling   the donkey is frightened

(a) Melons are falling out of the cart because

....

(b) People are covering their heads because

....

Why is smoke rising from the mountain?

Wildlife with Wings

Let's find out about how birds can fly. Complete the fun activities when you finish reading the story.

Animals that fly have wings. When birds fly, they move their wings forwards and down, then backwards and up. Many insects are also flyers. Bats are flying mammals. The picture shows a hummingbird. It can float, or hover, in the air in one spot. To do this, it moves its wings very quickly in different ways around its body. This helps the tiny hummingbird stay still enough to get to the sweet nectar inside flowers.

1 Read the story carefully and then read these sentences. Are they True (T) or False (F), or is there Not Enough Information (NEI) for you to decide? Colour in the star next to the correct answer.

(a) All animals have wings. ☆ T ☆ F ☆ NEI

(b) Nectar is found inside flowers. ☆ T ☆ F ☆ NEI

(c) Bats can hover. ☆ T ☆ F ☆ NEI

(d) Birds move their wings forwards and up. ☆ T ☆ F ☆ NEI

(e) All birds can fly. ☆ T ☆ F ☆ NEI

(f) A hummingbird can hover. ☆ T ☆ F ☆ NEI

2. Search the story for clues to the meaning of these words. Circle the correct answer.

(a) flyers

    birds that eat flies   birds that hover

    birds that fly

(b) hover

    to clean carpet   to talk loudly

    to stay still in the air

(c) nectar

    a sugary drink   a seed case

    rainwater

(d) float

    to sail   to fly   to drift

High Peaks

Read the story about mountains. Complete the fun activities when you finish reading the story.

In some parts of the world, mountains rise high into the air. Near the top of some mountains it is always cold. Snow covers them all through the year. Very few plants can grow near their peaks. The Matterhorn is a high mountain between Switzerland and Italy. Thirty of the highest mountain peaks in the world are in the Himalaya Mountains. This huge mountain range is in the far north of India. The world's highest mountain, Mount Everest, is in the Himalayas.

1. Match the jigsaw parts to make sentences. Use different colours to match the sentence parts.

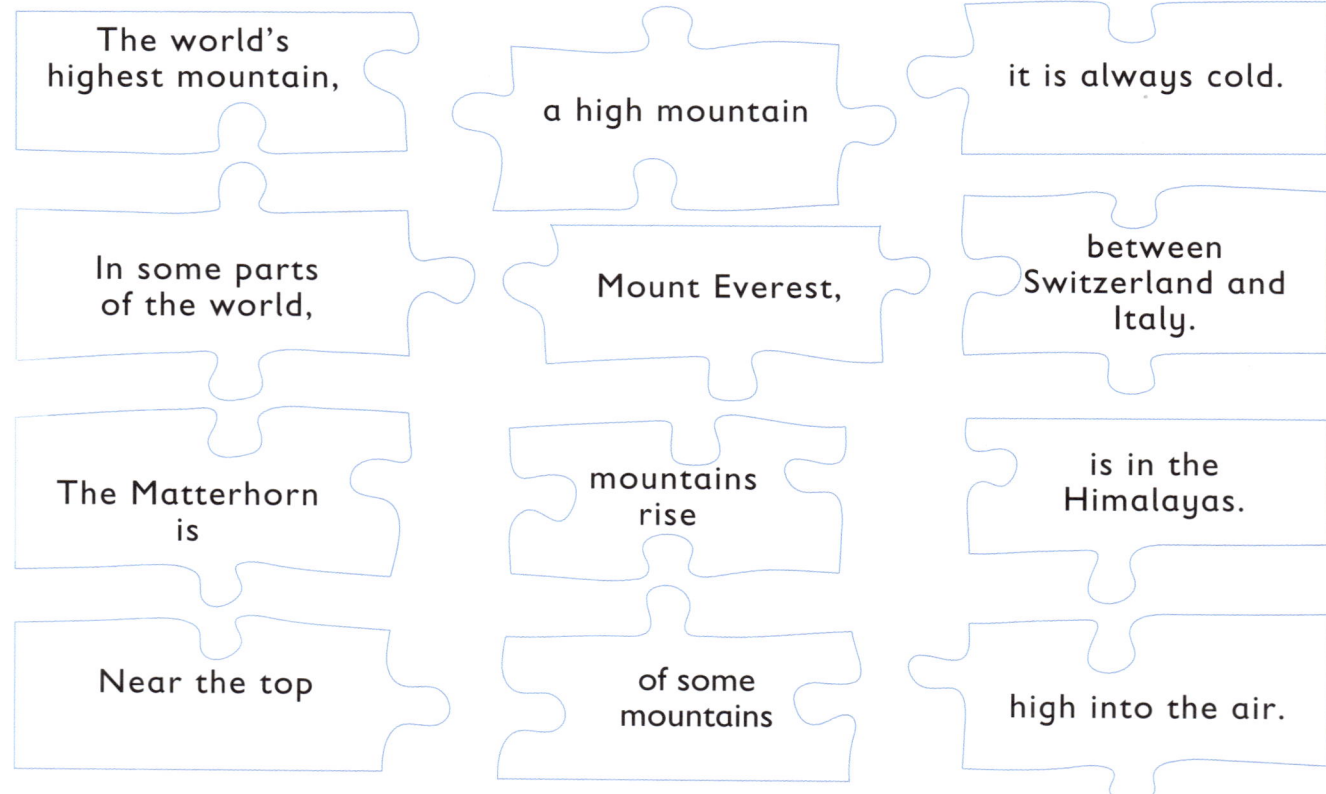

2   Read the story carefully and then read these sentences. Are they True (T) or False (F), or is there Not Enough Information (NEI) for you to decide? Colour in the star next to the correct answer.

(a) Switzerland is next to Italy. ☆ T ☆ F ☆ NEI

(b) Snow covers all mountain peaks. ☆ T ☆ F ☆ NEI

(c) Not many plants grow on snowy peaks. ☆ T ☆ F ☆ NEI

(d) The highest mountain in the world is the Matterhorn. ☆ T ☆ F ☆ NEI

(e) The Himalayas is the longest mountain range in the world. ☆ T ☆ F ☆ NEI

(f) Mount Everest is part of the Himalayas. ☆ T ☆ F ☆ NEI

3   Look at the following words and choose the ones that go with the words below.

library   fleet
range   string

(a) a .... of mountains
(b) a .... of beads
(c) a .... of books
(d) a .... of ships

Mount Everest

Working in Ancient Times

What do you know about everyday work in ancient Greece? Read this information about it. Use a dictionary to find the meaning of new words. Have fun trying the word puzzles, too.

Many ancient Greeks worked hard. Others, who were rich, did not need to earn a living. They owned slaves and paid labourers to work for them. Slaves are people who belong to someone else and are forced to work for them. Many slaves were captured in wars. Some slaves earned money and then paid to become free. In the picture, slaves and labourers are crushing grapes to make wine, by treading on them in vats.

1 Answer these questions about the story.

(a) What do we call a person who is owned by someone else?
....

(b) How did the Greeks find many slaves?
....

(c) Rich people did not work. Who did the work for them?
....

(d) What is meant by the phrase 'to earn a living'.
....

(e) How could a slave become free?
....

2 Which of these statements are facts and which are points of view (opinions). Write the word 'Fact' or 'Opinion' in each space.

(a) Rich people owned slaves. ....

(b) It is cruel to own slaves. ....

(c) I would not like to be a slave. ....

(d) Labourers in ancient Greece earned money. ....

(e) Children should not be made to work crushing grapes. ....

3 Look at the picture. Who might be saying this? Write the answer in the space.

My feet are all purple now. ....

Look! Can you get those big grapes? ....

My music will keep us happy. ....

I feel like a bird up here. ....

In go the grapes! ....

This basket gets heavier with each trip. ....

Harsh Places

Learn about a part of the world where it is hard for life to exist. Then complete the activities. They will help you discover more about the world around you.

In hot regions, food can be hard to find. In some places there is nothing to drink. Many animals have learnt to store food to eat later on. Camels in the desert store fat and moisture in humps on their back. Squirrels store nuts and seeds in hollow trees. Gerenuks live in dry parts of Africa. These animals never need to drink. In the picture, the gerenuks are getting moisture from leaves. They use their long neck to reach them.

squirrel

1   Answer these questions about the story.

   (a) Can you name three animals that live in harsh places?

   ....

   (b) How does a camel survive in the desert?

   ....

   (c) How does a squirrel survive in very cold places?

   ....

   (d) How does a gerenuk survive in dry parts of Africa?

   ....

camel

gerenuks

2 Uscramble these letters to make words from the story.

(a) stun .... (e) sleave ....

(b) manilas .... (f) eden ....

(c) deters .... (g) reset ....

(d) nerve .... (h) alert ....

3 Which animal is which?

Colour in the stars that fit the description of the animals.

	camel	gerenuk	squirrel
(a) lives in a harsh, dry place	☆	☆	☆
(b) lives in a harsh, cold place	☆	☆	☆
(c) is a large animal	☆	☆	☆
(d) can store extra food in its body	☆	☆	☆
(e) can store food in hiding places	☆	☆	☆
(f) has a long neck	☆	☆	☆
(g) has a bushy tail	☆	☆	☆

Space and the Solar System

Let's find out about planet Earth and our solar system in space. Complete the fun activities when you finish reading the story.

People, plants and animals live on Earth. They do not live on the other planets. Earth is one of eight planets in our solar system. These planets and other objects in space always move around a large star that we call the Sun. The solar system is part of the universe. Space is the word we use to mean everywhere in the universe. The universe has many millions of stars, moons and planets. It is growing bigger all the time.

1   Answer these questions about the story.

(a) Which is bigger, a country or planet Earth?

....

(b) Which is bigger, planet Earth or the solar system?

....

(c) Which is bigger, the solar system or the universe?

....

(d) Which is smaller, planet Earth or the universe?

....

2 Use the words in the list to fill in this no-clues crossword.

ASTEROID
COMET
EARTH
JUPITER
MARS
MERCURY
MOON
NEPTUNE
PLUTO
ROCKET
SATURN
SKY
SOLAR
SPACE
STAR
SUN
TELESCOPE
UNIVERSE
URANUS
VENUS

Moonwalk

Read the story about people who have walked on the Moon. If you find a new word, look at the words around it to help work out the meaning. Complete the fun activities when you finish reading the story.

Between 1969 and 1972, six *Apollo* spacecraft took people to the Moon. So far, 12 men have walked on the Moon. When they were there, they could take giant steps. This is because there is little gravity on the Moon. Gravity is a force that pulls things towards the centre of a planet or moon. When there is no gravity, everything just floats. In 1969, Neil Armstrong was the first man to stand on the Moon. In 1971, Alan Shepard went to the Moon on *Apollo 14*. He hit a golf ball. He said it went for 'miles and miles'.

1 Answer these questions about the story.

(a) Who was the first person to stand on the Moon?

....

(b) How many people have walked on the Moon so far?

....

(c) What is gravity?

....

(d) In space there is no gravity. What would happen to a ball in space?

....

2. The word 'moonwalk' is a compound word. It is made up of 'moon' + 'walk'. Split up each of these compound words.

(a) spacecraft = ... + ...
(b) footprints = ... + ...
(c) splashdown = ... + ...
(d) everything = ... + ...
(e) mankind = ... + ...

3. Unscramble these letters to make words from the story.

lopolA ....   tangi ....

varygit ....   fogl ....

lkawde ....   mono ....

What country's flag is flying near the module?

Tails Old and New

Read the story about lizards. Use a dictionary to find the meaning of new words. Complete the fun activities when you finish reading the story.

Lizards belong to a group of animals called reptiles. Lizards usually have a thin body and long tail. Most lizards can live for a short time without a tail. When it senses danger, a lizard can shed its tail. The rest of it can then escape. Soon, a new tail grows back to replace the one that was lost. The collared lizard in the picture on page 29 has a long, round tail. To escape from danger, this lizard lifts its tail in the air and runs on its back legs.

chameleon

1 Read the story and look at the pictures to help each lizard find its tail. Write the answers in the spaces below.

(a) My tail is curled into a spiral shape. ....

(b) My tail is short and wide with flat grey scales. ....

(c) My tail has lots of small spikes. ....

(d) My tail is blue with brown spots. ....

(e) My tail is long and narrow with lots of small scales. ....

Australian shingleback

leaf-tailed gecko

skink

2 Answer these questions about the story.

(a) Why does a lizard shed its tail?

....

(b) How does the collared lizard escape from danger?

....

(c) What happens soon after a lizard has shed its tail?

....

3 Fill in the no-clues crossword with these names of lizards.

ANOLE
BASILISK
CHAMELEON
COLLARED
FRILLED
GECKO
IGUANA
KOMODO
SKINK
TUATARA

collared lizard

The Roller Coaster

What do you know about roller coasters? Read the story. If you find a new word, look at the words around it to help work out the meaning.

Most new inventions are helpful to people. Some inventions are just for fun. A roller coaster is scary fun. Cars speed along twisting steel tracks. They climb up high and plunge suddenly and steeply down. They even turn upside down. Computers control the cars' speed and movement. The cars' wheels are firmly clamped to the track. The people are strapped inside.

1 Answer these questions about the story.

(a) Why was the roller coaster invented?

....

(b) How are the cars' speed and movement controlled?

....

(c) Why don't people fall out of the car when it turns upside down?

....

(d) Have you been on a roller-coaster ride?
Think of four words to describe the feeling.

....

2 Here is an example of a word ladder. It takes two steps to turn the word 'wall' into the word 'tail'. Only one letter can be changed in each row.

wall – change one letter (w to t)
tall – change one letter (l to i)
tail – Hooray!

w	a	l	l
t	a	l	l
t	a	i	l

Now it's your turn.

(a) Change the word 'car' into the word 'fun'.
Fill in the table with the words.
Only one letter can be changed in each row.

c	a	r
f	u	n

(b) Turn the word 'roll' into the word 'ride'.
Fill in the table with the words.
Only one letter can be changed in each row.

r	o	l	l
r	i	d	e

track

car

Making a Mummy

Let's find out how ancient Egyptians made mummies. Complete the fun activities when you finish reading the story.

To stop a dead body from rotting, ancient Egyptians turned it into a mummy. They believed that the soul of the mummy would last forever. The liver, lungs, stomach, brain and intestines were taken out and put in special jars. Then the body was dried out. The body was then wrapped in bandages and oil and put into a coffin. A priest was in charge of making a mummy. He wore a mask like a jackal's head in honour of the god Anubis, the god of mummy-making.

1. Answer these questions about the story.

    (a) Why did ancient Egyptians turn a dead body into a mummy?

    ....

    (b) Who was the god of mummy-making?

    ....

    (c) Name the person who was in charge of mummy-making?

    ....

2. Are these **sentences True** or False? Colour in the star next to the **correct answer**.

(a) A body usually rots after death. ☆ True ☆ False

(b) A jackal is a type of fish. ☆ True ☆ False

(c) A mummy can last for a very long time. ☆ True ☆ False

3. Number these steps on how to make a mummy in the correct order.

.... Wrap the body in bandages.

.... Remove the lungs, liver and brains.

.... Put the body in a coffin.

.... Dry the body out.

4. Unscramble these words to make words from the story.

(a) Unscramble 'pots' to make a word that means 'to halt'.

....

(b) Unscramble 'slung' to make a word that is part of the body.

....

(c) Unscramble 'salt' to make a word that is the opposite of 'first'.

....

Sneaky Spiders

Here is some information about a sneaky spider.
Read the story. Try to sound out new words.
Then enjoy completing the activities.

A trapdoor spider lives in a hole, or burrow, under the ground. The burrow has a door spun from silk. The spider pushes the door open to catch its victim. Some trapdoor spiders make the burrow door very strong by mixing earth with the silk. In this picture, a giant centipede is breaking into a trapdoor spider's burrow. But the spider is hiding in a secret room that has a silk door.

1   Answer these questions about the story.

(a) Where does a trapdoor spider live?

....

(b) What is the spider's door made from?

....

(c) How does a trapdoor spider make the door very strong?

....

2. Make up a speech balloon for the trapdoor spider and the giant centipede in the picture.

trapdoor spider

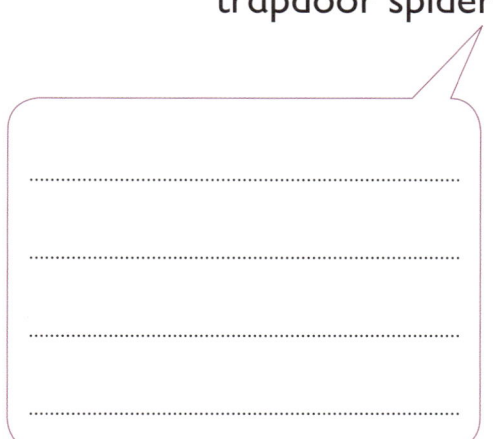

giant centipede

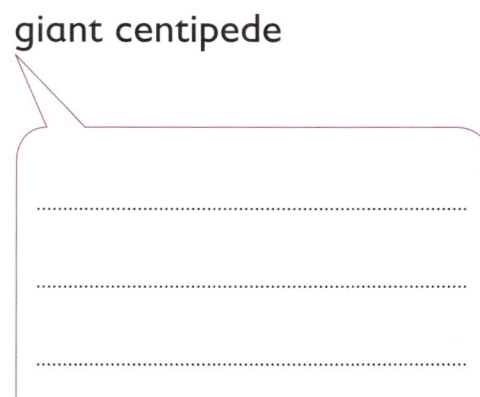

centipede

trapdoor spider

3. Use the letters of the word 'SPIDER' to fill in this sudoku. Each letter appears once in each line across and down, and once in each mini-grid.

		S		P	I
	I				
			D		E
D					
S					
E	R		P	I	

Making the Moon

Do you know how the Moon was made? Read the story and find out. Try to sound out new words. Then enjoy completing the activities.

Not long after Earth was formed, it was hit by an asteroid. When the asteroid hit Earth, the surface of our planet was still covered with hot, melted rock. Broken rocks were hurled out into space. They formed a ring around Earth. Gradually, they joined together to make the Moon. The area of the whole of the Moon's surface is the same as the area of the continent of Africa.

1. Answer these questions about the story.

    (a) Which continent has the same area as the surface of the Moon?

    ....

    (b) Which formed first, Earth or the Moon?

    ....

    (c) Which is smaller, Earth or the Moon?

    ....

    (d) Do you think dinosaurs were alive when the Moon was formed? Why or why not?

    ....

2 Search the story for clues to the meaning of these words. Circle the correct answer.

(a) asteroid

    muscle   rock in space   a moon   a star

(b) hurled

    thrown   shipped   formed   mixed up

(c) gradually

    evenly   quickly   slowly   sadly

3 Number these sentences in the correct order.

Broken rocks were flung into space. ....

An asteroid hit Earth. ....

Earth was formed. ....

Broken rocks joined together to make the Moon. ....

Broken rocks formed a ring around Earth. ....

No More

Here is some information about animals that no longer exist in our world. Read the story. Try to sound out new words. Then enjoy completing the activities.

Many kinds of animals that once lived no longer exist. The pictures show two animals that used to live in polar regions. Snow and ice always cover the ground in these cold parts of the world. Great auks were birds that could not fly. People hunted them for food and to use as bait for fishing. That is why they finally disappeared. About 120,000 years ago, mammoths lived on icy plains. These huge animals died out when the weather got warmer.

great auk

1 Use the story to finish these sentences.

  (a) Snow and ice always cover the ground in ....

  (b) .... were birds that could not fly.

  (c) Great auks disappeared because people ....

  (d) The mammoth died out when ....

  (e) The .... and the .... are two animals that no longer live.

2. Look closely at the picture. Colour the stars that fit the description.

	mammoth	great auk
(a) can fly	☆	☆
(b) has wings	☆	☆
(c) has tusks	☆	☆
(d) has large ears	☆	☆
(e) no longer exists	☆	☆

3. Can you help the great auk find its way through the maze to get to its home?

mammoth

Dino Babies

Read the story about dinosaur babies. If you find a new word, look at the words around it to help work out the meaning.

Dinosaurs lived on Earth long before there were any people. Many were huge. Others were very small animals. Just like birds, dinosaurs made nests and laid eggs. Baby dinosaurs hatched from these eggs. Many dinosaurs cared for their babies in the nests. They fed them until they could walk. The mother *Oviraptor* in the picture is feeding her babies with another kind of baby dinosaur that she has caught.

1 Use the words from the group below to complete the paragraph.

| fed | eggs | nests |
| birds | dinosaurs | until |

Long ago, dinosaurs made .... and laid .... just like .... do today. Baby .... hatched from these eggs. Mother dinosaur .... her baby dinosaurs. She looked after them .... they could walk.

2 Read the story carefully and then read these sentences. Do you Agree (A) or Disagree (D)? Colour in the star next to the correct answer.

(a) Dinosaurs are alive today. ☆ A ☆ D

(b) *Oviraptor* laid eggs. ☆ A ☆ D

(c) There were very large dinosaurs long ago. ☆ A ☆ D

(d) There were small dinosaurs long ago. ☆ A ☆ D

(e) *Oviraptor* did not eat meat. ☆ A ☆ D

(f) Dinosaurs laid only one egg. ☆ A ☆ D

(g) Mother dinosaurs looked after young dinosaurs. ☆ A ☆ D

(h) People kept dinosaurs as pets. ☆ A ☆ D

3 Look at the picture. Who might say this?

Lunch is ready. ....

That looks yum, Mum! ....

Help! ....

Inventions at Home

What do you know about the inventions you use at home? Read this information about them. Try the word puzzles, too.

Many inventions make our life easier and more comfortable. Can you imagine not having a refrigerator? Until about 60 years ago, most people used ice to cool food. Large blocks of ice were delivered to homes every day. A flush toilet is another helpful invention. Water flows from the cistern into the bowl. Then it washes out through the S-bend. More water fills up the cistern to be ready for the next time.

1. Choose the best phrase from below to finish each of these sentences.

> to cool food   the S-bend of the toilet
> 60 years ago   were delivered to homes
> from the cistern to the bowl

(a) Large blocks of ice ....

(b) Most people used ice ....

(c) In a flush toilet, water flows ....

(d) Refrigerators were invented about ....

(e) Water washes out through ....

2 Can you imagine not having a refrigerator?
   How would life be different? Write down some examples.
   Think about ice cream, meat, milk, hot days, ice storage.

   ....

   ....

3 Search the word puzzle for the words below and circle them.

BROOM
COMPUTER
FAN
FREEZER
HEATER
KNIFE
LAMP
LOCK
MATCHES
NOTEBOOK
OVEN
PENCIL
PIN
RADIO
SHOWER
SOAP
TOILET
UMBRELLA
TELEVISION

```
          J R I
          N K       C H W O L
          N O T E B O O K
          I       R A D I O
          F
      M F A N   E     L A M P
    S A T E L E V I S I O N X
  P H T U M B R E L L A F V O P
  I O C O M P U T E R P R V E F
  N W H Z Z K B G T K E E A Y N
  E E E C L D B O R N E Q V M
  R S O A I P E I C C Z F O
    L O R T R P L I I E O
      F A C E V E W L R
        M P Q R T R B
```

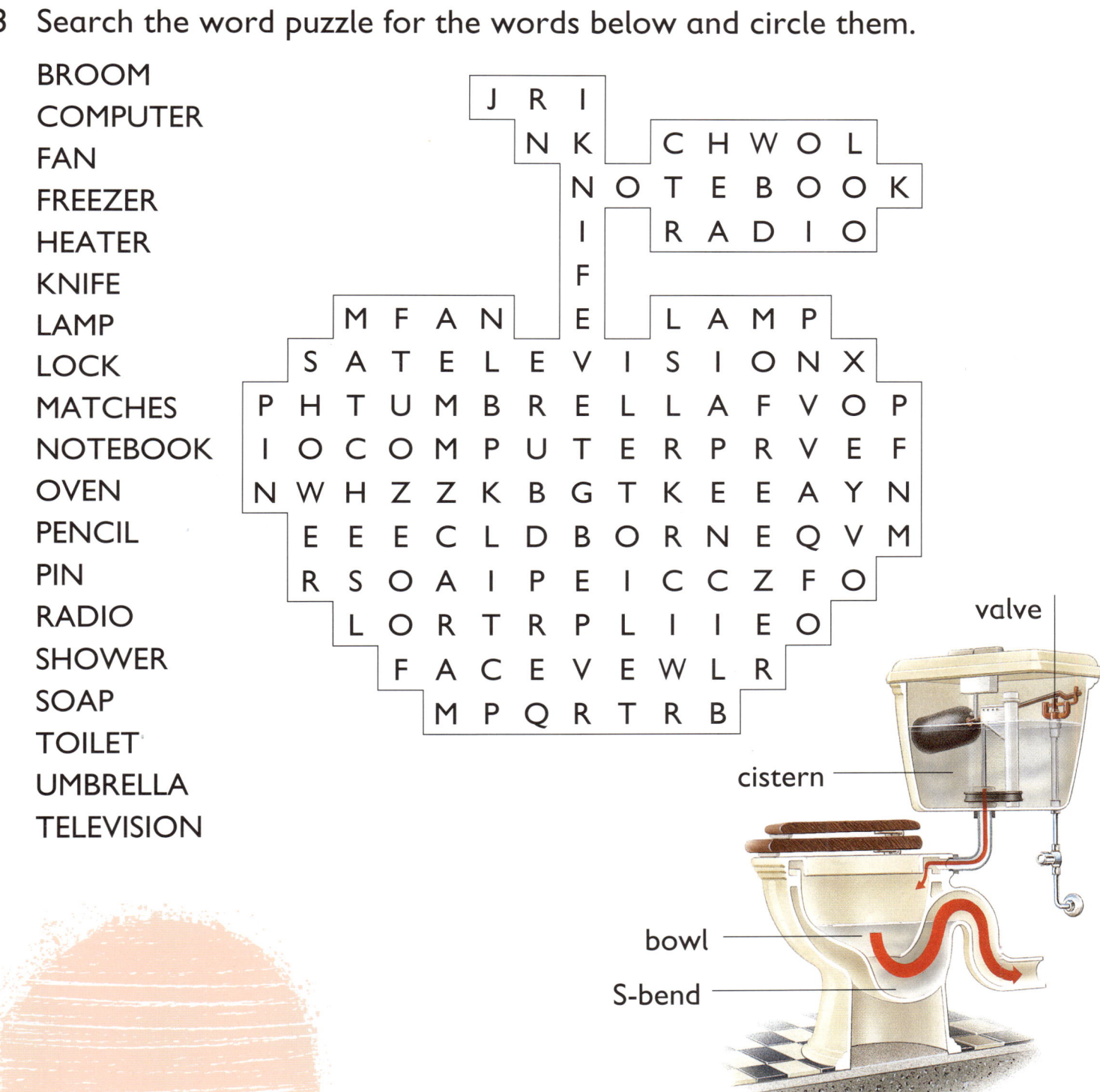

valve
cistern
bowl
S-bend

43

Bright Colours

Learn about lizards and how they hide. Then complete the activities. They will help you discover more about the world around you.

A lot of lizards are dull grey or brown. Many others are brightly coloured. Some lizards have colourful patterns. A lizard's colour can help it to hide from animals that want to attack it. The colourful pattern that helps an animal to hide is called camouflage. The blue-tailed day gecko lives on an island in the Indian Ocean. It feeds mainly on insects and nectar that it gets from flowers.

1   Which lizard said this? Was it A, B or C?

   (a) I have thick dark brown stripes down my back.
       I am a five-lined skink.   ....

   (b) I am light green with brown stripes and dots.
       I am an Italian wall lizard.   ....

   (c) My tail is orange, but my body is green and black.
       I am a dwarf flat lizard.   ....

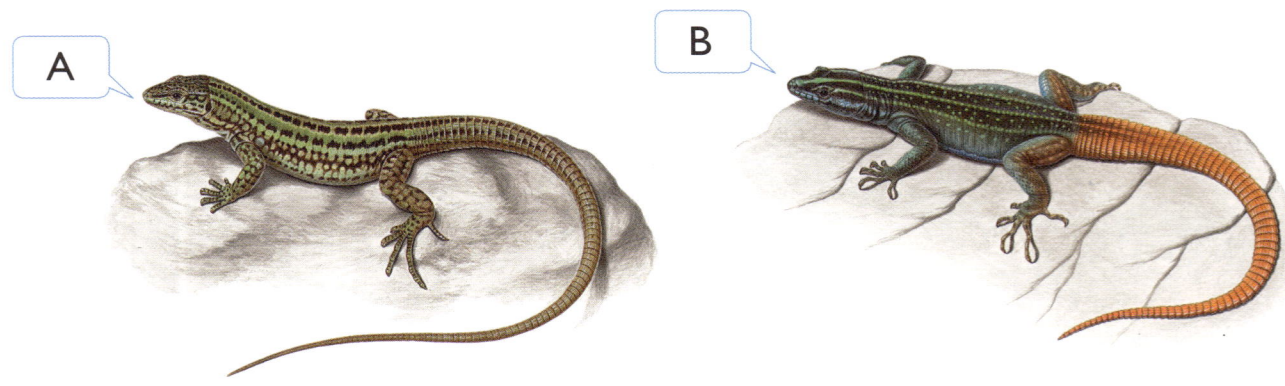

2 Read the story carefully, look at the pictures and then read these sentences. Are they True (T) or False (F), or is there Not Enough Information (NEI) for you to decide? Colour in the star next to the correct answer.

(a) Camouflage makes it easy for animals to hide. ☆ T ☆ F ☆ NEI

(b) The blue-tailed day gecko is dull grey. ☆ T ☆ F ☆ NEI

(c) There are no lizards on islands. ☆ T ☆ F ☆ NEI

(d) The dwarf flat lizard eats insects and nectar. ☆ T ☆ F ☆ NEI

(e) A lizard will attack a snake. ☆ T ☆ F ☆ NEI

3 Have a look at page 31 for an example of a word ladder.

Now it's your turn.

Change the word 'five' into the word 'dove'.
Fill in the table with the words.

f	i	v	e
d	o	v	e

C

blue-tailed day gecko

Reef Hunters

Let's find out about hunters that live on a coral reef. If you find a new word, look at the words around it to help work out the meaning.

Coral reefs exist in shallow seas in warm parts of the world. Lots of colourful fish live there. A coral reef looks like a peaceful garden, but there are hunters lurking there. Sharks attack large fish. Larger fish feed on small ones. Octopuses catch crabs, and jellyfish sting their prey. The grey reef shark is just one of the several sharks that hunt on reefs. Different sharks catch different fish, so they do not compete for food.

1 Which is which? Look at the picture and read the story. Colour the stars that fit the description.

	shark	jellyfish	sponge	clownfish	octopus
(a) has colourful stripes	☆	☆	☆	☆	☆
(b) stings its prey	☆	☆	☆	☆	☆
(c) has fins	☆	☆	☆	☆	☆
(d) attacks large fish	☆	☆	☆	☆	☆
(e) catches crabs	☆	☆	☆	☆	☆
(f) lives on a coral reef	☆	☆	☆	☆	☆

2 Search the word puzzle for the words in the list below
   and circle them.

CLOWN
CORAL
CRABS
FISH
GREY
HUNTERS
JELLY
OCTOPUS
PREY
REEF
SEA
SHARK
SPONGE
STING

```
                                    H F H
            I D R              C C U I U D F
            P E E            G L O N S R D A E
            E I D          E R O R T H S B ■ R F
            F C R A B S E W A E Z H H R P G E
              S T I N G Y N L R C A T B Y Y T A
              S P O N G E L U D S N R H Z M D S
              S E A       P R E Y T C K B D F I
            Q W T             J E L L Y L M Q Y
          O E J               O C T O P U S
                                F L L
```

Tornado!

What do you know about tornadoes and twisters? Read this information about them. Use a dictionary to find the meaning of new words. Try the word puzzles, too.

Tornadoes are huge funnels of wind and cloud. They move across the ground at great speed. Like giant vacuum cleaners, they suck up trees and buildings. Rain, thunder and lightning come with them. Tornadoes twist upwards, so people often call them twisters. A tornado that forms over water is called a waterspout. Tornadoes occur in many parts of the world, but a large number of them happen in parts of the United States.

1. Read the story carefully and then read these sentences. Are they True (T) or False (F), or is there Not Enough Information (NEI) in the story for you to decide? Colour in the star next to the correct answer.

   (a) Another name for a tornado is a twister. ☆ T ☆ F ☆ NEI

   (b) There are twisters in Italy. ☆ T ☆ F ☆ NEI

   (c) Rain, thunder and lightning are called twisters. ☆ T ☆ F ☆ NEI

   (d) Tornadoes are made of falling wind and cloud. ☆ T ☆ F ☆ NEI

   (e) Tornadoes do not only happen on land. ☆ T ☆ F ☆ NEI

   (f) The largest tornadoes occur in the United States. ☆ T ☆ F ☆ NEI

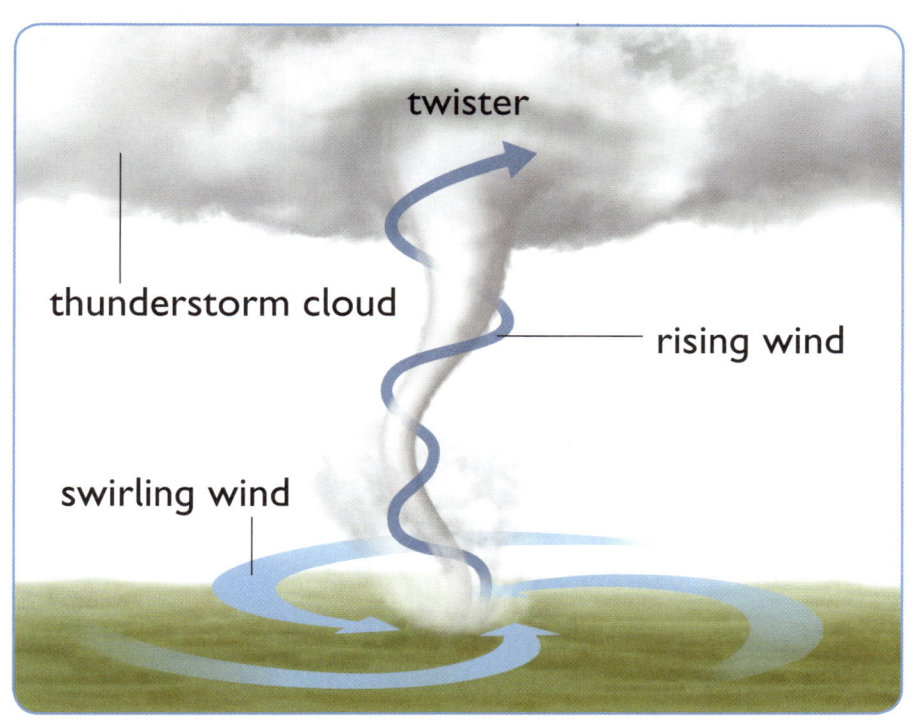

> Say this 10 times, no mistakes: Tasty Twister.

2. Find the opposite of these words and phrases in the story. Write them in the spaces.

(a) spit out ....

(b) tiny ....

(c) downwards ....

(d) under ....

(e) small number ....

3. What am I?

My first letter is in 'crew' but not in 'brew'.
My second letter is in 'clap' but not in 'cap'.
My third letter is in 'slow' but not in 'slew'.
My fourth letter is in 'fourth' but not in 'forth'.
My fifth letter is in 'dray' but not in 'ray'.

I am a ....

All about Helicopters

Here is some information about how a helicopter works. Read the story. Try to sound out new words.

Helicopters can go straight up and straight down. They can also float in the air or hover. They can fly forwards, backwards and sideways. All helicopters have turning blades called rotors. The rotors control how fast and which way the machine will go. Helicopters can get to places that aeroplanes cannot reach. Helicopters are able to rescue people. The helicopter in the picture hovers as it saves a man after an accident far out at sea.

1. Read the story and then complete these activities.

    (a) Colour the stars that show the ways that a helicopter can fly.

    ☆ up   ☆ upside down   ☆ down   ☆ forwards
    ☆ flip   ☆ backwards   ☆ underwater

    (b) What are the turning blades on top of the helicopter called?

    ....

    (c) In what way is a helicopter better than an aeroplane?

    ....

    (e) What word means to float in the air?
    Colour the star next to the correct answer.

    ☆ rescue   ☆ blades   ☆ turning   ☆ hover

2 **What am I?**

My first letter is in 'cat' but not in 'hat'.
My second letter is in 'hoot' but not in 'soot'.
My third letter is in 'cove' but not in 'cave'.
My fourth letter is in 'chip' but not in 'chin'.
My fifth letter is in 'pet' but not in 'vet'.
My sixth letter is in 'pet' but not in 'pot'.
My last letter is in 'break' but not in 'beak'.

This is another word for helicopter.

I am a ....

3 Read the story and write the words that rhyme with:

(a) brown   ....
(b) boat   ....
(c) last   ....
(d) faces   ....
(e) patrol ....

straight up

straight down

forwards

sideways

St Basil's Cathedral

Here is some information about the great building called St Basil's Cathedral in Moscow, Russia. Read the story. Try to sound out new words. Then complete the activities.

Some great buildings in the world are centuries old. In 1554, in Moscow, Russia, work began on St Basil's Cathedral. It was built to celebrate Russia's victory in a war. The church was named after a holy man called Basil the Blessed. This colourful building was first painted white. Can you see the domes shaped like onions? Moscow is very cold in winter. There are lots of heavy snowfalls. Snow slides easily off these domes.

1 Spot the differences between these two pictures. Picture B has seven differences.

   ....
   ....
   ....
   ....
   ....
   ....

A — central tower
  — onion dome

2. Here's a fun crossword. The answers are words in the story.

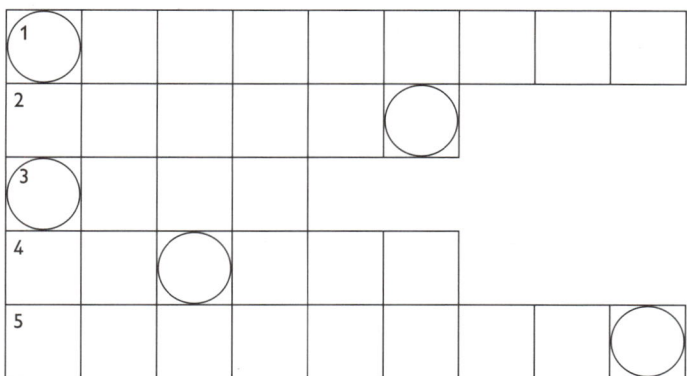

1. St Basil's is one of the world's great ....
2. Moscow is found in this country.
3. Moscow gets large falls of this in winter.
4. The domes of St Basil's are shaped like these.
5. Another name for a grand church.

3. Who am I? Write down the circled letters from the crossword.

....

B

School in Ancient Times

Read the story about going to school in ancient Greece. If you find a new word, look at the words around it to help work out the meaning.

In ancient Greece only sons of rich parents went to school. Boys at school learnt reading, writing and arithmetic. They wrote with pointed sticks on wooden boards that were covered with wax. Boys learned to play a musical instrument called the lyre, which had strings, and pipes, which they blew into like a flute. Some girls learnt reading and writing at home. When they were 18, young men were taught to fight, so they could be soldiers.

1. Were the ancient Greeks just like us, or were they different? Read these sentences and decide whether they were the Same or Different. Colour in the star under the correct answer.

	Same	Different
(a) Boys learnt reading, writing and arithmetic.	☆	☆
(b) Only sons of rich parents went to school.	☆	☆
(c) They wrote with sticks on wax boards.	☆	☆
(d) Girls did not go to school.	☆	☆
(e) Boys learnt to play the lyre.	☆	☆
(f) At 18, young men were taught how to fight.	☆	☆

2 Have a look at page 31 for an example of a word ladder.

Now it's your turn.

(a) Change the word 'pen' into the word 'pal'.
Fill in the table with the words.
Only one letter can be changed in each row.

p	e	n
p	a	l

(b) Change the word 'kit' into the word 'bag'.
Fill in the table with the words.
Only one letter can be changed in each row.

k	i	t
b	a	g

3 Which words in the story mean the opposite of these words?
Circle the correct answer.

(a) rich

poor   wealthy   unhappy

(b) ancient

fresh   old   modern

(c) pointed

blunt   sharp   jagged

Long Horns

Learn about reindeer and their antlers. Then complete the activities. They will help you discover more about the world around you.

Some animals and humans live in very cold places. Reindeer, or caribou, live in the cold regions near the North Pole. They eat leaves, mosses and grasses. They have large horns called antlers that grow on their head. The antlers grow in spring and fall off in winter. Skin covers the antlers during summer. A reindeer's foot has four toes. When the reindeer walks on soft snow, the toes spread out to give a better grip.

1. Answer these questions about the story.

    (a) What is an antler?

    ....

    (b) Where in the world do reindeer live?

    ....

    (c) In which season do a reindeer's antlers fall off?

    ....

    (d) It is hard to walk on snow. How does the reindeer do this?

    ....

2 Use the words from the group below to fill in the missing words.

> Pole   summer   horns   fall
> live   grow   winter

Reindeer have long .... called antlers. In winter the antlers .... off. In spring the antlers begin to .... In .... , skin covers the antlers until they drop off again in .... Reeindeer .... near the North .... in very cold regions.

3 Draw the reindeer's antlers in summer. You can copy the picture.

spring   summer

autumn   winter

antler

reindeer

toe

The Sun

Read the story about the Sun in our solar system. If you find a new word, look at the words around it to help work out the meaning.

The Sun belongs to a galaxy, or huge group of stars, called the Milky Way. The Sun is at the centre of our solar system. It provides light and heat for Earth. The Sun is a huge mass of burning hydrogen and other gases. It is nearly 5 billion years old. We call the centre of the Sun the core. The outside part is the corona. Sunspots are cooler, dark parts of the Sun.

1. Search the story for clues to the meaning of these words. Circle the correct answer.

    (a) galaxy

    rocks and asteroids   group of stars   outer space

    (b) sunspot

    cooler part of the Sun   hot part of the Sun   core of the Sun

    (c) core

    part of an apple   group of soldiers   centre

    (d) corona

    type of car   outside part of the Sun   desert animal

2 Look at the words and choose the ones that go with the words below.

| dog | Moon | butter | saucer |
| gold | pepper | chair | fork |

(a) Sun and .... (e) salt and ....
(b) knife and .... (f) table and ....
(c) bread and .... (g) cup and ....
(d) silver and .... (h) cat and ....

3 Use the words to complete the paragraph.

| galaxy | solar system | heat |
| light | outside | core |

The Milky Way is the name of a .... Our Sun is part of that galaxy. It is also the centre of our .... Life on Earth gets both .... and .... from the Sun. The .... edge of the Sun is the corona. The centre of the Sun is the ....

Giant Plant-eater

What do you know about the dinosaur *Stegosaurus*? Read this information about it. Use a dictionary to find the meaning of new words. Try the word puzzles, too.

Dinosaurs lived for 160 million years. They died out about 65 million years ago. While many dinosaurs ate other animals, most of them fed mainly on plants. *Stegosaurus* was a giant plant-eater. It had no front teeth. It had a beak that it used to chop off clumps of ferns. *Stegosaurus* had bony plates on its neck, back and tail. These helped to keep it warm or cool. It could use the spikes on its tail to defend itself.

1 Write a question to match each answer.

   (a) Question: ....
       Answer: It used the spikes to defend itself.

   (b) Question: ....
       Answer: It chopped plants off with its beak.

   (c) Question: ....
       Answer: 65 million years ago.

   (d) Question: ....
       Answer: They helped to keep *Stegosaurus* warm or cool.

   (e) Question: ....
       Answer: I would feel scared, but not afraid of being eaten.

2   Which is the odd one out? Circle the correct answer.

(a) *Stegosaurus*   *Tyrannosaurus*   walrus

(b) meat-eater   plant-eater   eggbeater

3   Can you help *Stegasaurus* find its way through the maze to get to its home?

bony plate

sharp spike

The Roman Senate

Here is some information about the ancient Roman Senate. Read the story. If you find a new word, look at the words around it to help work out the meaning. Then enjoy completing the activities.

The Senate was a group of important men who ruled ancient Rome. The men were called senators. Romans voted for senators each year. Only men were allowed to vote. Only a man could be a senator. They met together at a special place called the Curia. Here they made new laws. In the picture, you can see the senators sitting on benches. In later years, an emperor was in charge of the Senate. In this picture, Emperor Titus is hearing news about a disaster at the city of Pompeii.

1 Answer these questions about the story.

   (a) Name the place where ancient Roman senators met.

   ....

   (b) How often were senators elected to the Senate?

   ....

   (c) Who was in charge of the Senate in later years?

   ....

2 Spot the differences between these two pictures.
Picture B has eight differences.

....
....
....
....

The Titanic

Read the story about an ocean liner called the *Titanic*. Complete the activities when you finish reading the story.

> The *Titanic* was a luxurious ship. She was said to be very safe. In April 1912 she left the United Kingdom for New York, USA. There was great excitement as the huge liner sailed from port. Four days later, the *Titanic* hit an iceberg and sank. The night when the *Titanic* sank was very calm, but very dark. By the time the lookouts saw the iceberg, there was not enough time for the *Titanic* to avoid hitting it. The *Titanic* sank, along with more than two-thirds of the 2,223 people on board. The wreck was found 73 years later.

1 Answer these questions about the story.

(a) Why did the *Titanic* sink?

....

(b) Why didn't the lookouts see the iceberg?

....

(c) What year was the *Titanic* rediscovered?

....

(d) If 1,517 people died, how many survived?

....

2 Can you help the *Titanic* find her way through the maze to get to land?

land

> What looks like white mountains in the picture?

The Sinking of the *Titanic*

What do you know about the sinking of the *Titanic*? Read this information about it. Use a dictionary to find the meaning of new words. Try the word puzzles, too.

In 1912 the *Titanic* sailed on her maiden voyage from Southampton, UK, to New York, USA. The *Titanic* was said to be nearly unsinkable, but she struck an iceberg. The lifeboats were loaded with women and children first. However, most of the people on board were lost. The pictures show how the boat filled with water. The bow of the *Titanic* went down first. The rest of the ship broke up and sank. Fewer than three hours after the collision, the ship was gone.

1. Read the story carefully and then read these sentences. Are they True (T) or False (F), or is there Not Enough Information (NEI) for you to decide? Colour in the star next to the correct answer.

   (a) Everyone survived on the *Titanic*. ☆ T ☆ F ☆ NEI
   (b) The *Titanic* was unsinkable. ☆ T ☆ F ☆ NEI
   (c) It was the captain's fault that the *Titanic* sank. ☆ T ☆ F ☆ NEI
   (d) The *Titanic* struck an iceberg. ☆ T ☆ F ☆ NEI
   (e) It took about three hours for the ship to sink. ☆ T ☆ F ☆ NEI
   (f) There weren't enough lifeboats for everyone. ☆ T ☆ F ☆ NEI

2 Look closely at the pictures. Then number the sentences in the correct order.

.... The hull breaks apart.

.... Water enters the bow and holes for the anchor.

.... The ship finally sinks.

.... The *Titanic* is sinking bow first. A funnel is lost.

3 Here's a fun crossword. The answers are words in the story or on this page.

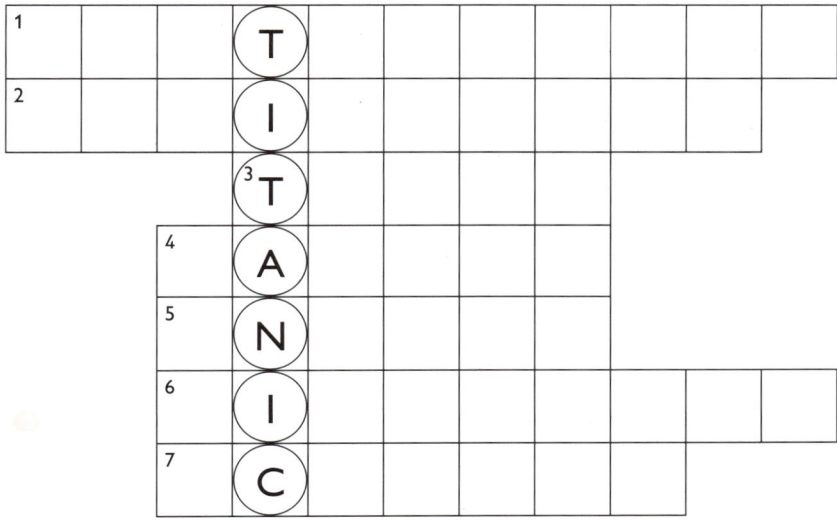

1. The *Titanic* left from this English port.

2. Cannot sink.

3. Number of hours it took for the *Titanic* to sink.

4. The first voyage made by a ship.

5. It stops a ship from floating away.

6. Small boats stored on a big boat to help people escape.

7. The *Titanic* hit this and sank.

bow

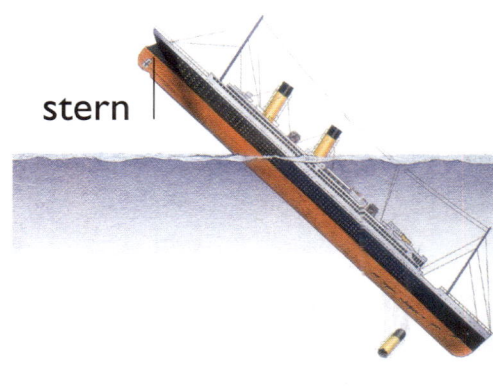
stern

Hot-air Balloons

Let's find out about how a hot-air balloon works. Complete the fun activities when you finish reading the story.

People have always dreamt of being able to fly. For more than 200 years, people have been flying in hot-air balloons. Burners heat air or gas inside the balloon. It is then lighter than the air outside. The balloon lifts up and is driven by wind currents. When a balloon pilot pulls a rope called a ripcord, hot air escapes. As heavier cold air replaces the hot air, the balloon moves down towards the ground.

1. Read the story carefully and then read these sentences. Are they True (T) or False (F), or is there Not Enough Information (NEI) for you to decide?
   Colour in the star next to the correct answer.

   (a) People have been flying in balloons for 200 years. ☆ T   ☆ F   ☆ NEI

   (b) Cold air can make a balloon move down. ☆ T   ☆ F   ☆ NEI

   (c) Hot air makes a balloon move down. ☆ T   ☆ F   ☆ NEI

   (d) Wind currents help a balloon to fly. ☆ T   ☆ F   ☆ NEI

   (e) It is not difficult to pilot a hot-air balloon. ☆ T   ☆ F   ☆ NEI

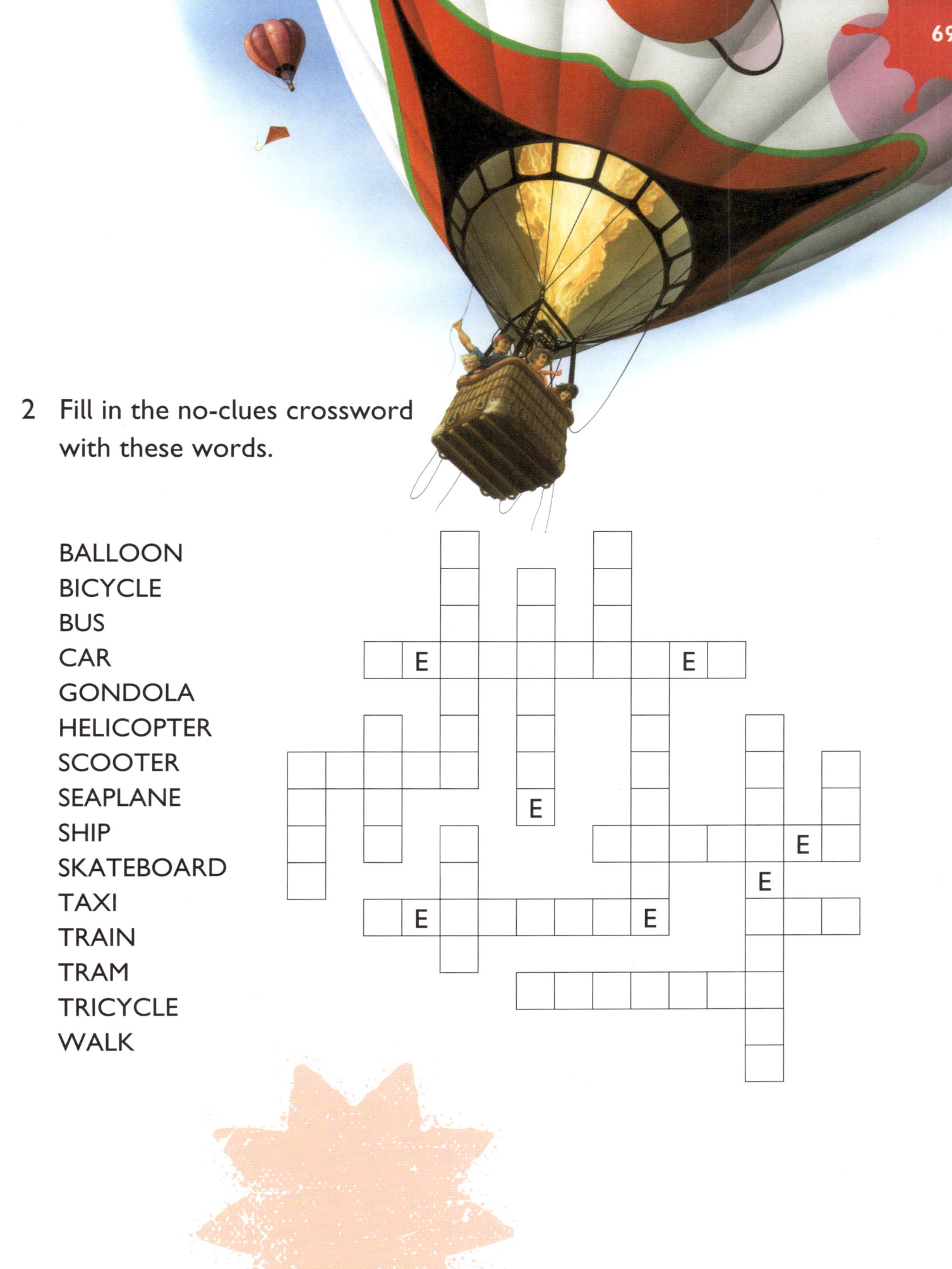

2. Fill in the no-clues crossword with these words.

BALLOON
BICYCLE
BUS
CAR
GONDOLA
HELICOPTER
SCOOTER
SEAPLANE
SHIP
SKATEBOARD
TAXI
TRAIN
TRAM
TRICYCLE
WALK

Danger Looms

Here is some information about scary lizards.
Read the story. Try to sound out new words.
Then enjoy completing the activities.

There are many animals that attack lizards for food. Most lizards have a way of scaring off attackers. Some hiss loudly. Some have coloured tongues to make themselves look scary. Some lizards can make themselves look bigger when they are in danger. The Australian frilled lizard hisses and puffs out the frill behind its neck. Most lizards move along the ground on four legs. The frilled lizard can run fast on its two hind legs.

1 Use the story and the picture to complete these activities.

(a) List three ways that a lizard can scare off attackers.

....

(b) How does the Australian frilled lizard scare away predators?

....

(c) How does the blue-tongued lizard scare away predators?

....

(d) When it escapes from danger, how many legs does a frilled lizard use?

....

frilled lizard

blue-tongued lizard

2 Circle the correct words to complete each sentence.

Snakes and lizards belong to a ...group / groupe.. of animals called reptiles. Most lizards have a way of ..scareing / scaring.. off attackers. Some make a ..loud / lowd.. hiss. Some lizards make themselves look scary with a coloured ..tongue / tungue.. The Australian frilled lizard puffs out the ..frill / fwill.. behind ..its / it's.. neck.

3 What group of animals do lizards belong to? Colour in the star next to the correct answer.

☆ reptiles   ☆ mammals   ☆ amphibians

4 Colour in the star next to the word that is the odd one out.

(a) ☆ lizard   ☆ snake   ☆ spider

Why? ....

(b) ☆ blue   ☆ red   ☆ frill

Why? ....

(c) ☆ danger   ☆ risk   ☆ safety

Why? ....

Everyday Life in Pompeii

Here is some information about everyday life in Pompeii. Have fun with the word puzzles and activities when you finish reading the story.

In the first century, Pompeii was a rich and lively city in western Italy. Many of the people of Pompeii were wealthy. They lived in large, fine houses called villas and wore rich clothes. They could live like this partly because they had slaves to do all the work. Wealthy people ate fancy meals with many courses. One special meal was roast peacock with live birds inside. When the peacock was carved at the table the birds would fly out.

1. Here are some questions about the story. Colour in the star next to the correct answer.

    (a) Where was the city of Pompeii?
    ☆ northern Italy ☆ southern France ☆ western Italy

    (b) Which people lived in villas in Pompeii?
    ☆ everyone ☆ rich people ☆ poor people

    (c) Why could many of the people of Pompeii live in such a fancy way?
    ☆ they ate fancy meals ☆ they loved expensive clothes
    ☆ they had slaves to do all the work

2. Number these instructions in the right order for a roast peacock recipe.

.... Remove peacock from oven.

.... Put peacock in the oven.

.... Place three small live birds inside cooked peacock.

.... Watch the little birds fly out.

.... Take peacock to the table and carve.

.... Roast peacock for 1 hour.

3. Draw a peacock like the one in the illustration. Colour it in.

Can you spot the sports champion getting a prize?

Telling Time

Learn about how time is measured. Have fun with the word puzzles and activities when you finish reading the story.

About 3,500 years ago Egyptians used water clocks to measure the hours at night. They used two pots. Water dripped through a hole from one pot to another. Markings on the side of the pot showed how much water had dripped through and how many hours had passed. In the day, they could tell the time by where the Sun was in the sky. Today we use wristwatches, which were invented in 1907. Newer, digital watches display numbers.

wristwatch

1. Look closely at the pictures of the water clock. Answer these questions about the story in the spaces below.

    (a) What happened to the water in pot 1, and why?

    ....

    (b) What happened to the water in pot 2?

    ....

    (c) How did the time scale markings on the side of pot 2 tell the time?

    ....

    (d) What was used to tell the time during the day?

    ....

2. Read the story carefully and then read these sentences. Are they True (T) or False (F), or is there Not Enough Information (NEI) for you to decide?
Colour in the star next to the correct answer.

(a) Water clocks were used during the day. ☆ T ☆ F ☆ NEI
(b) Time is easy to measure. ☆ T ☆ F ☆ NEI
(c) It is possible to tell the time by the Sun. ☆ T ☆ F ☆ NEI
(d) Digital watches have hands that move. ☆ T ☆ F ☆ NEI
(e) Egyptians were clever people. ☆ T ☆ F ☆ NEI

3. Draw a line from the riddle questions to the correct answers.

When do clocks die?	Time.
What kind of clock is crazy?	A watchdog.
How does a witch tell the time?	When their time is up.
What flies without wings?	A cuckoo clock.
What animal keeps the time?	With a witch watch.

time scale markings

pot 1

pot 2

Military Aircraft

Here is some information about military aircraft.
Use a dictionary to find the meaning of new words.
Try the word puzzles, too.

Aeroplanes have been important in the wars of the last century. Military aircraft fight each other in the air. They drop bombs on enemy positions. Aeroplane designers are always inventing new wing shapes that will help aircraft to fly faster. The bottom aeroplane on page 77 has a very strange shape. It has thin, pointed surfaces. This makes the aircraft hard to see on radar screens. Radar can pick up the speed and position of things like planes.

1   Answer these questions about the story.

(a) What is the job of a military aeroplane?

....

(b) Why do airplane designers make up new wing shapes?

....

(c) The bottom aeroplane on page 77 is very unusual. Why?

....

(d) List some other ways we use aeroplanes.

....

(e) Why is radar a useful tool?

....

2 Search the word puzzle for the words in the list below and circle them.

AIR
BALLOON
BIRD
CABIN
COCKPIT
ENGINE
FUEL
PERISCOPE
PLANE
PRESSURE
ROTOR
RUDDER
WING

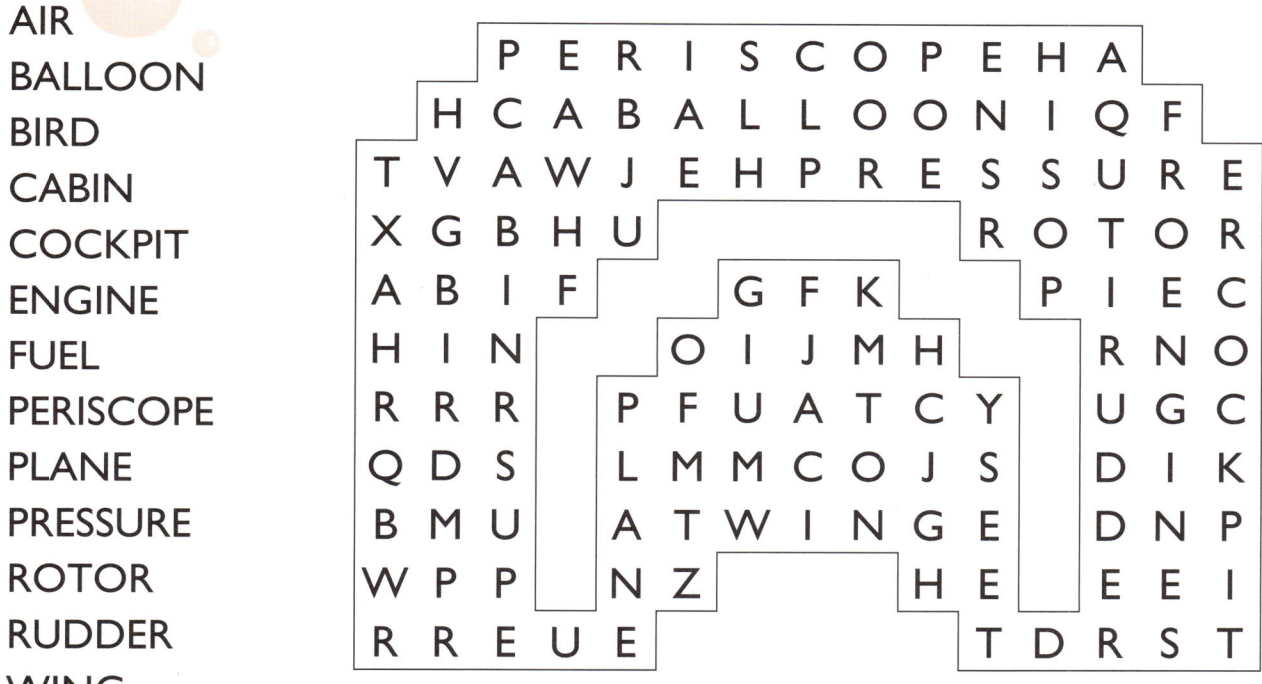

		P	E	R	I	S	C	O	P	E	H	A		
	H	C	A	B	A	L	L	O	O	N	I	Q	F	
T	V	A	W	J	E	H	P	R	E	S	S	U	R	E
X	G	B	H	U						R	O	T	O	R
A	B	I	F			G	F	K			P	I	E	C
H	I	N			O	I	J	M	H			R	N	O
R	R	R		P	F	U	A	T	C	Y		U	G	C
Q	D	S		L	M	M	C	O	J	S		D	I	K
B	M	U		A	T	W	I	N	G	E		D	N	P
W	P	P		N	Z				H	E		E	E	I
R	R	E	U	E						T	D	R	S	T

delta wing
swept-forward wing
swept-back wing
short, thin wing
swing-wing

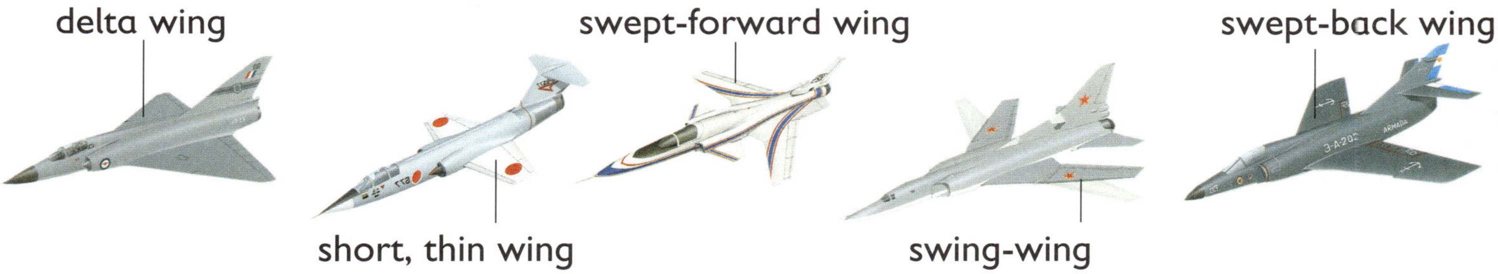

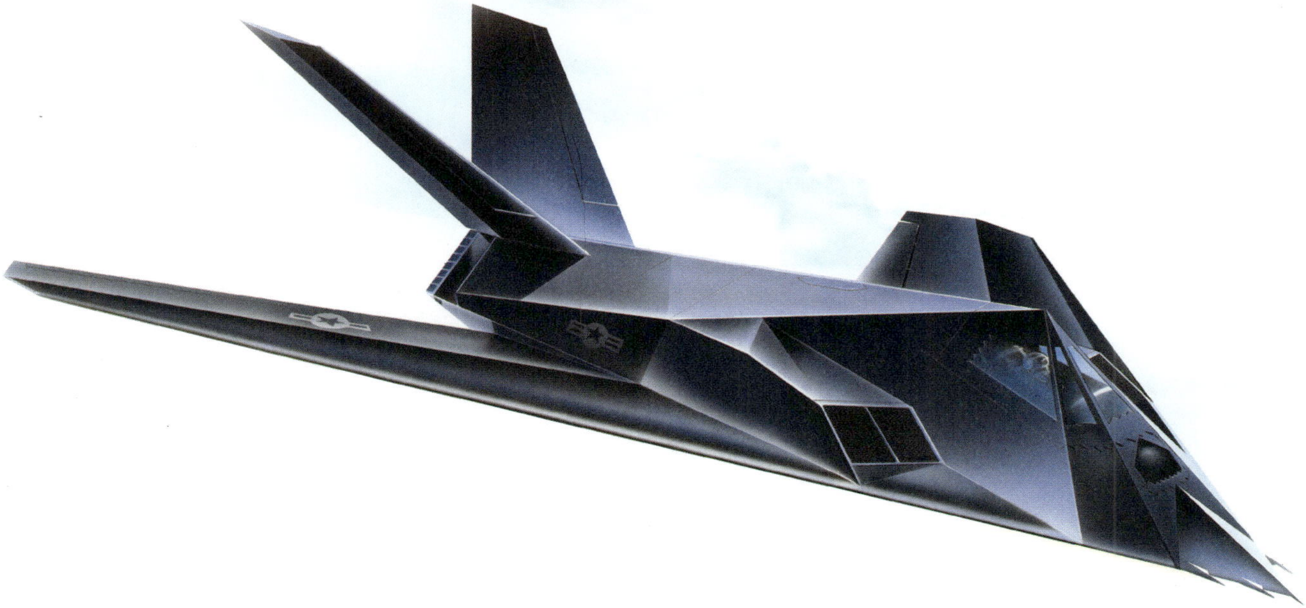

Safe Homes

What do you know about a beaver's home?
Use a dictionary to find the meaning of new words.
Try the activities, too.

Beavers live in parts of North America and Europe. They spend a lot of time in the water. They make large ponds by building dams in rivers. They build their homes in the middle of the ponds. Beavers' homes are called lodges. They are made from logs, branches and stones. In their lodges, beavers are safe from wolves and bears that attack them. They enter and leave the lodges through tunnels.

1   Read the story carefully and then read these sentences. Are they True (T) or False (F), or is there Not Enough Information (NEI) for you to decide?
    Colour in the star next to the correct answer.

   (a) Beavers live in part of South America.   ☆ T   ☆ F   ☆ NEI
   (b) Lodges are found in the middle of ponds. ☆ T   ☆ F   ☆ NEI
   (c) Beavers can breathe under the water.   ☆ T   ☆ F   ☆ NEI
   (d) Tunnels are the only way to get into a lodge. ☆ T ☆ F ☆ NEI
   (e) Beavers are dangerous animals.   ☆ T   ☆ F   ☆ NEI

2. Fill in the missing letters in these sentences.

Be......vers can bui......d a lod......e in t......e mid......le of a ......ond. Here t......ey are sa......e fro...... ......ears a......d w......lv......s.

3. Search the story for clues to the meaning of these words. Colour in the star next to the correct answer.

(a) pond
☆ puddle   ☆ river   ☆ pool

(b) lodge
☆ home   ☆ underneath   ☆ trunk

(c) enter
☆ include   ☆ go in   ☆ go out

☆ Why is the beaver chewing the tree?

Star Gazing

Here is some information about the night sky. Try to sound out new words. Then enjoy completing the activities.

On a clear night, the sky is full of light. If you look at the sky, you can see thousands of stars. They are a small part of the Milky Way. One of the brightest lights is Venus, a planet that glitters like a star. You can see more stars if it is dark. Lights in cities can block out a lot of your view. People who study the planets and stars now use huge radio telescopes. The large dishes pick up signals from space.

radio telescopes

1   Complete these sentences by choosing the correct words from below. Write your answers in the spaces provided.

Way	Venus	stars
radio	night	Milky
dish	dark	block

On a clear .... you can see thousands of .... They are part of the .... It is easier to see more stars if it is .... Bright city lights can .... out the view. One of the brightest lights is the planet .... People who study stars and planets use a .... telescope with a large .... to pick up signals from space.

2. A code is a system of signals or symbols used to send messages.

In this code, you can tell which letter is being used by the lines and symbols that go with it.

A	B	C
D	E	F
G	H	I

J*	K*	L*
M*	N*	O*
P*	Q*	R*

S**	T**	U**
V**	W**	X**
Y**	Z**	

For example, in this code, the word 'night' is:

N. I. G. H. T.

Now use the code to work out these words.

....

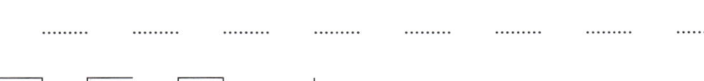

....

....

3. Tonight, look at the sky. Draw what you see.

Dangerous Icebergs

Let's find out about icebergs. Complete the fun activities when you finish reading the information.

A glacier is a solid river of ice. Icebergs are large pieces of freshwater ice that have broken off glaciers or ice shelves. The icebergs then float out to sea. Only the tip of an iceberg shows above water. It is hard to know how much is hidden. In 1912 a large ship, the *Titanic*, hit an iceberg and sank. The iceberg's sharp edges made gashes in the ship's side. Most of the people on board died.

above water

underwater

1 Search the story for clues to the meaning of these words. Colour in the star next to the correct answer.

(a) solid
☆ hard   ☆ bursting   ☆ full

(b) hidden
☆ nest   ☆ buried   ☆ visible

(c) gashes
☆ dashes   ☆ shadows   ☆ cuts

(d) float
☆ cork   ☆ drift   ☆ sink

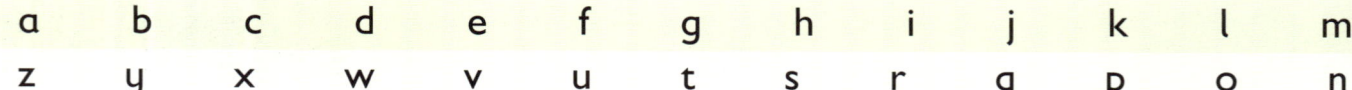

2. A code is a system of signals or symbols used to send messages.

In this code, the real letters are replaced by different letters. Look closely at the key at the bottom of this page, solve the secret code questions, then answer them (not using code).

Here is an example:

Question: Are you a top reader?
Question (in code): Ziv blf z glk ivzwvi?
Answer: Yes, I am a top reader.

(a) Question in code: Dszg rh zm rxvyvit?

Answer: ....

(b) Question in code: Dsb rh rg sziw gl pmld gsv hrav lu zm rxvyvit?

Answer: ....

(c) Question in code: Dszg rh z tozxrvi?

Answer: ....

(d) Question in code: Dsviv dlfow blf urmw zm rxvyvit?

Answer: ....

the *Titanic*

gashes

n	o	p	q	r	s	t	u	v	w	x	y	z
m	l	k	j	i	h	g	f	e	d	c	b	a

Sydney Opera House

Let's find out about the great building called the Sydney Opera House. Complete the fun activities when you finish reading the story.

Many buildings in the world are grand and impressive. Some are old buildings and some are new. Between 1958 and 1973 a new building slowly grew on the shores of Sydney Harbour, in Australia. It is made of remarkable concrete shells that are covered with white tiles. They look like the sails of boats on the water. Inside the Sydney Opera House is a large hall where concerts are held. There are also several theatres.

1. Write your own questions to match these answers.

    (a) Question: ....
    Answer: Between 1958 and 1973.

    (b) Question: ....
    Answer: It is made of remarkable concrete shells covered with tiles.

    (c) Question: ....
    Answer: Like the sails of boats on the water.

2. Which words in the story mean the opposite of these words? Write your answers in the spaces provided.

    (a) few .... (d) quickly ....

    (b) unimpressive .... (e) black ....

    (c) old .... (f) small ....

3 Here's a fun crossword. The answers are words in the story.

Across

1. ancient
2. pleasing
3. big
4. edges of a harbour
5. a number of

white tiles

At Home in Ancient Greece

What do you know about life in ancient Greece? Have fun with the word puzzles and activities when you finish reading the story.

Greek houses had walls of mud bricks. Their roofs were made of pottery tiles. In the centre of a house was an open courtyard. In this courtyard was an altar where the family prayed to their gods. Rich people had male and female slaves who helped them with the cooking and all the other housework. Greeks wore garments called tunics. These were large pieces of material that they wrapped around their body. Can you see people in the house with tunics on?

1. Read the story carefully and then read these sentences. Are they True (T) or False (F), or is there Not Enough Information (NEI) for you to decide?
   Colour in the star next to the correct answer.

   (a) Greeks prayed to their gods in the courtyard. ☆ T ☆ F ☆ NEI

   (b) At home Greeks wore only bath towels. ☆ T ☆ F ☆ NEI

   (c) Ancient Greeks had pets at home. ☆ T ☆ F ☆ NEI

   (d) Rich people had slaves to help them. ☆ T ☆ F ☆ NEI

   (e) Greek houses were made of concrete. ☆ T ☆ F ☆ NEI

   (f) Tunics did not keep people warm in winter. ☆ T ☆ F ☆ NEI

2 Look closely at the picture. What are people doing in each of these rooms?

(a) Room A ....
(b) Room B ....
(c) Room C ....
(d) Room D ....
(e) Room E ....
(f) Room F ....

Leafy Seadragons

What do you know about leafy seadragons? Read this information about them, then try the fun word puzzles.

A leafy seadragon is very hard to see in the water. Its fins are like leaves. Seadragons blend in with the seagrass and seaweed that surround it. This is called camouflage. Other animals cannot find or attack it. A seadragon's long mouth is like a tube. Through this tube, a seadragon sucks in tiny sea creatures. It swallows them whole. Female seadragons lay their eggs on a male's tail. The eggs stay there for six weeks until they hatch.

1 Answer these questions about the story.

(a) What sort of environment does the seadragon live in?
    Colour in the star next to the correct answer.
    ☆ rocks   ☆ sand   ☆ seagrass

(b) Why is a seadragon very hard to see in the water?

....

(c) How does a seadragon eat its food?

....

(d) Where do seadragon eggs remain until they hatch?

....

2. The word 'seadragon' is a compound word. It is made up of 'sea' + 'dragon'. Make up compound words from the words below.

(a) stone + fish = ...

(b) clown + fish = ...

(c) sea + grass = ...

(d) jelly + fish = ...

3. Search the word puzzle for the animal words in the list below and circle them.

ANEMONE
CHAMELEON
CLOWNFISH
CROCODILE
GECKO
MANTIS
SEADRAGON
SHRIMP
TIGER
ZEBRA

```
            Z
          C E N
        Z N B Q B
      R O C R L L I
    E M H Q A I Z S M
  G E J V Z F M R Z A X
I N C H A M E L E O N X K
T A G E C K O U D V N T M P U
  C R O C O D I L E W I V Y
    C L O W N F I S H S D
      S E A D R A G O N
        S H R I M P Q
          U H E D E
            I G S
              J
```

leafy seadragon

Sea and Wind Power

Let's find out about how the sea and wind shape the land. Complete the fun activities when you finish reading the story.

Earth's surface is shaped by the power of the sea and wind. Water in seas and oceans is never still. Often, huge waves beat against the land. This wears away beaches and rocks and pushes coastlines inland. Winds, too, can carve out new shapes in the rocks like the arch in this photo. As the sea wears away a cliff, caves form. Slowly, caves turn into arches. Finally, an arch loses its top to become a sea stack.

1 Answer these questions about the story.

(a) Name two natural powers that shape the land.

....

(b) How is the coastline pushed inland?

....

(c) What is the name of the type of wind-shaped rock in the photo?

....

2 Number these sentences in the correct order.

.... Finally, an arch loses its top to become a sea stack.

.... As the sea wears away a cliff, caves form.

.... Slowly, caves turn into arches.

3 Colour in the star next to other things that help to shape the land.

☆ earthquakes ☆ rivers ☆ magic ☆ humans ☆ glaciers
☆ volcanoes ☆ fire ☆ music ☆ hurricanes

sea cave

sea arch

sea stack

4 Here is an example of a word ladder. It takes two steps to turn the word 'wall' into the word 'tail'. Only one letter can be changed each row.

wall – change one letter (w to t)
tall – change one letter (l to i)
tail – Hooray!

w	a	l	l
t	a	l	l
t	a	i	l

Now it's your turn.

Change the word 'wind' into the word 'land'.
Fill in the table with the words.
Only one letter can be changed in each row.

w	i	n	d
l	a	n	d

Moon Base

Read the story about setting up a Moon base. If you find a new word, look at the words around it to help work out the meaning.

In July 1969 astronauts landed and walked on the Moon for the first time. Now there are plans to set up a Moon base where astronauts can live and work. They could get water from the ice at the Moon's south pole. Solar panels would make electricity from the heat of the Sun. Scientists also want to send astronauts to Mars. It is a very long way away. The astronauts would have to stay on Mars for more than a year.

1. Answer these questions about the story.

    (a) What exciting plans are there for the Moon?

    ....

    (b) Where would astronauts get fresh water?

    ....

    (c) How could astronauts get electricity?

    ....

    ....

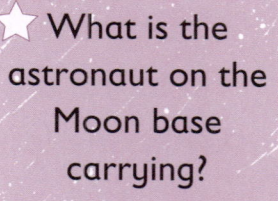

What is the astronaut on the Moon base carrying?

2. Search the story for clues to the meaning of these words. Colour in the star next to the correct answer.

(a) solar
   ☆ of the Sun   ☆ energy   ☆ fire

(b) lunar
   ☆ night time   ☆ of the stars   ☆ of the Moon

(c) base
   ☆ a square   ☆ a station   ☆ a tent

3. Design your own Moon base. It needs to have living space, water storage, solar panels for electricity and a lunar rover.

The Dinosaur Disappears

Learn more about why dinosaurs disappeared. Complete the fun activities when you finish reading the story.

Scientists believe that 65 million years ago a huge meteorite hit our Earth. A meteorite is a large piece of rock or metal that comes from outer space. Vast amounts of dust flew into the air. The dust blocked out the Sun. Most plants and animals need sunlight to live. Many experts agree, therefore, that the meteorite caused the death of the dinosaurs. A few believe that Earth's climate became much hotter and this is why they died.

1 Answer these questions about the story.

(a) What do many experts think caused the death of the dinosaurs?

....

(b) What is the other reason that some people believe caused the dinosaurs to disappear?

....

(c) What is a meteorite?

....

2. Do these pairs of sentences have the Same (S) meaning or a Different (D) meaning? Colour in the star next to the correct answer.

(a) (i) Dust flew into the air and blocked out the Sun.
(ii) The Sun was blocked out by dust. ☆ S ☆ D

(b) (i) The Earth became hotter 65 million years ago.
(ii) It is hotter today than it was 65 million years ago. ☆ S ☆ D

(c) (i) Most animals and plants need sunlight to live.
(ii) It needs to be sunny every day for plants and animals to live. ☆ S ☆ D

(d) (i) I love dinosaurs best of all animals.
(ii) Dinosaurs are my favourite animals. ☆ S ☆ D

Reefs and People

Let's find out about how people affect coral reefs. Have fun with the word puzzles and activities when you finish reading the story.

Corals have many shapes and colours. Many sea creatures live among them. People enjoy coral reefs for their beauty. But some of the things humans do can damage reefs. Soil from farms chokes coral. Substances, such as oil, in the water are also harmful. Many scientists now study coral reefs and the creatures that live among them. Using modern diving gear, they can watch corals and fish at very close quarters.

rubbish left on a reef

1 Which of these statements are facts and which are points of view (opinions)?
   Write the words 'Fact' or 'Opinion' in the spaces.

   (a) Humans don't care about coral reefs. ....

   (b) Corals have many shapes and colours. ....

   (c) Oil and soil are harmful for corals. ....

   (d) Humans should not get too close to coral reefs. ....

   (e) Scientists now study coral reefs very closely. ....

2. Here's a fun crossword. Read the story and find words that mean the same as these words or have a similar meaning.

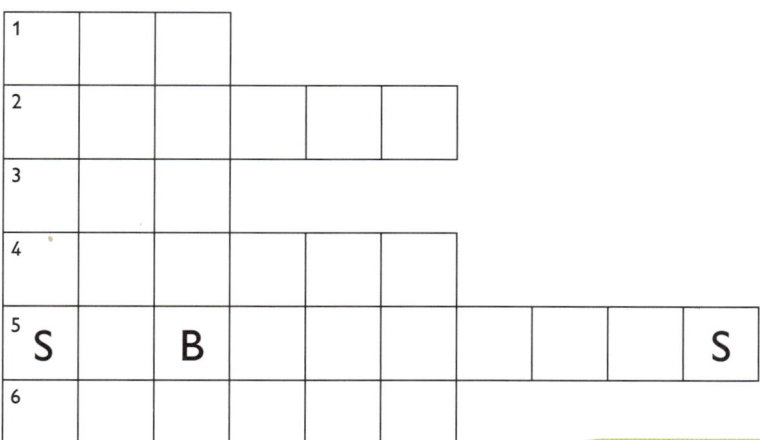

1. the ocean
2. smothers or stifles
3. grease
4. to harm
5. chemicals
6. good looks

3. What sort of coral fish am I?

My first letter is in 'tall' but not in 'ball'.
My second letter is in 'crave' but not in 'cave'.
My third letter is in 'thorough' but not in 'through'.
My fourth letter is in 'fourth' but not in 'forth'.
My last letter is in 'foot' but not in 'fool'.

I am a coral …… …… …… …… …… .

Warning Signs of a Volcano

What do you know about the volcano eruption at Pompeii, in Italy? Use a dictionary to find the meaning of new words. Try the word activities, too.

In AD 79 the volcano Mount Vesuvius erupted. It buried the city of Pompeii killing many of the people. Pompeii was a fine town with many shops and fountains. The people loved to visit the marketplace and public baths. Sometimes Pompeiians noticed small earthquakes. A few days before the volcano erupted, cracks appeared in stone walls. Some of the water fountains stopped flowing. Some paving broke on the roads. Some roof tiles fell off houses. People were uneasy, but not afraid. Then disaster struck.

1. Read the story carefully and then read these sentences. Are they True (T) or False (F), or is there Not Enough Information (NEI) for you to decide?
   Colour in the star next to the correct answer.

   (a) Mount Vesuvius is a volcano. ☆ T ☆ F ☆ NEI

   (b) Pompeiians were war-like people. ☆ T ☆ F ☆ NEI

   (c) Vesuvius erupted in the first century. ☆ T ☆ F ☆ NEI

   (d) Pompeiians knew Vesuvius would erupt. ☆ T ☆ F ☆ NEI

2. Look carefully at the picture. List two of the volcano warning signs that you can see.

3 Read these groups of words below and circle the odd word out in each group.

(a) sometimes　　always　　occasionally　　now and then

(b) erupt　　burst　　explode　　crack

(c) earthquake　　tremor　　flood　　shaking

(d) uneasy　　still　　peaceful　　quiet

4 Design a sign to warn people about the volcano.

Hunters and Fishers

Read the story about the Inuit people. If you find a new word, look at the words around it to help work out the meaning.

Inuit people live in icy northern regions of Alaska and Canada. They used to hunt using a spear at the end of a rope, called a harpoon. Now they use rifles. Inuit used to make clothes from the skin and fur of seals and deer. They also hunted these animals for food. In earlier times, Inuit people travelled across the ice and snow on sledges that were pulled by teams of dogs. Most Inuits now use snowmobiles, which have motors.

snowmobile

1 Answer these questions about the story.

(a) Where in the world do the Inuit people live?

....

(b) It is very cold in northern regions. How did Inuit keep warm?

....

(c) Can you think of some reasons why Inuit now use snowmobiles instead of teams of dogs?

....

....

2 Look closely at the picture of the Inuit fishing. Colour in the stars next to the words that describe him.

☆ sandshoes ☆ sandals
☆ dress ☆ snow boots
☆ gloves ☆ shoes
☆ beard ☆ T-shirt
☆ curly hair ☆ straight hair
☆ fur jacket ☆ warm trousers
☆ glasses ☆ shirt with buttons
☆ cap ☆ fur hood

3 Which of these statements are facts and which are points of view (opinions)?
Write the word 'Fact' or 'Opinion' in each space.

(a) Temperatures are very cold in the northern parts of Earth. ....

(b) Inuit must like cold weather. ....

(c) Hunting seals and deer is cruel. ....

(d) The snowmobile has replaced the dog team. ....

(e) Harpoons are better for hunting than rifles. ....

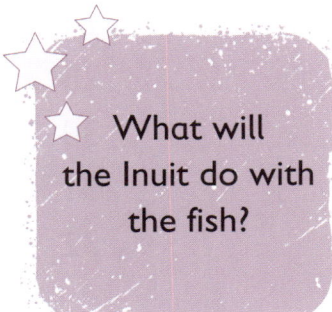

☆ What will the Inuit do with the fish?

Inuit fishing

Chapters of History

Here is a list of chapters for the story of the sinking of the *Titanic*. Read it, then complete the activities.

In April 1912, the passenger ship *Titanic* struck an iceberg and sank. Less than a third of those on board survived. The wreck of the *Titanic* was not found until 1985. The Contents page below lists the chapters of a book about this disaster. The page numbers show you where to read about each part of the story.

Contents

Construction	4
The Unsinkable *Titanic*	6
On Board	8
Luxury	10
The Route	12
The Collision	14
Icebergs	16
Evacuation	18
Sinking	20
Headline News	22
Survivors	24
Rediscovery	26
Relics	28
Quiz	30
Glossary	31
Index	32

Use the Contents page to answer the following questions.

1. On what page do these chapters start?

    (a) The Collision ....

    (b) Construction ....

    (c) Evacuation ....

2. What chapters start on these pages?

    (a) page 24 ....

    (b) page 16 ....

3. In which chapters would you find pictures of people in lifeboats?

    ....

4. What would you read about on page 26?

    ....

    ....

5. Which happened first? Colour in the star next to the correct answer.

    ☆ Headline News   ☆ The Collision   ☆ Evacuation

6. How many chapters of the story are there? Colour in the star next to the correct answer.

    ☆ 13 chapters   ☆ 16 chapters   ☆ 15 chapters

7. What items in the Contents are not chapters in the story?

    ....

passenger

Going to the Moon

Read the story about the first astronauts to land on the Moon. Have fun with the word puzzles and activities when you finish reading.

In July 1969, the *Apollo 11* spacecraft took astronauts to the Moon for the first time. Rockets helped it to take off and fly into space. As one part of a rocket ran out of fuel, it dropped off. The astronauts landed on the Moon in a vehicle called a lunar module. The main *Apollo 11* spacecraft went into orbit around the Moon while it waited for them to return. Only the tip of the original spacecraft returned to Earth.

1. Use the story and the picture to number these events in the right order.

   .... Spacecraft starts to return.

   .... Blast off!

   .... Lunar module lands on the Moon.

   .... First part drops off.

   .... Splash down!

   .... Spacecraft arrives at the Moon.

   .... Second and third parts drop off.

Second part drops off.

2. Can you help the spacecraft find its way through the maze to get back to Earth?

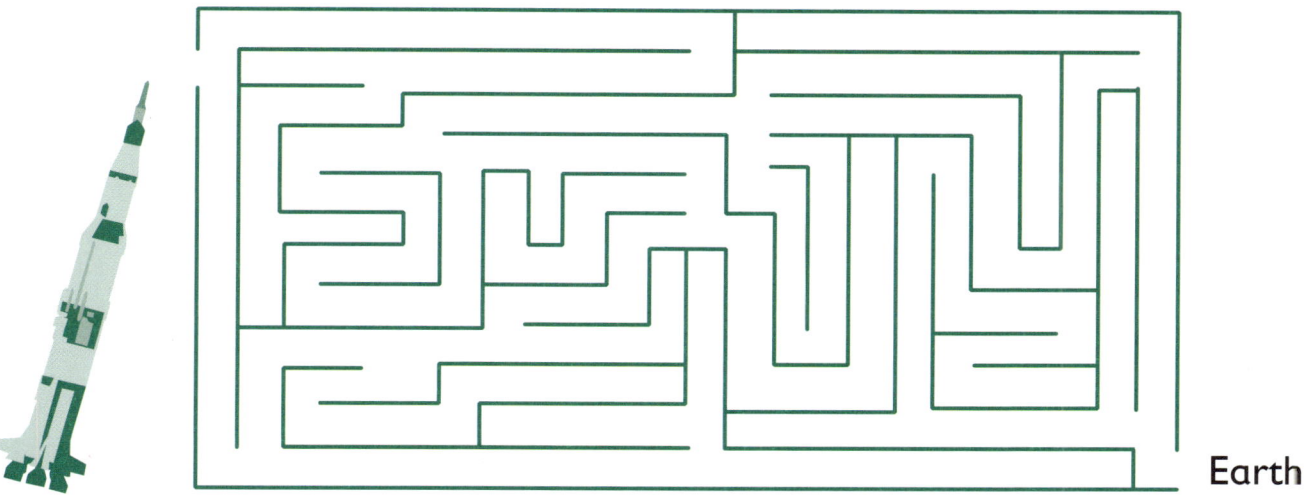

Earth

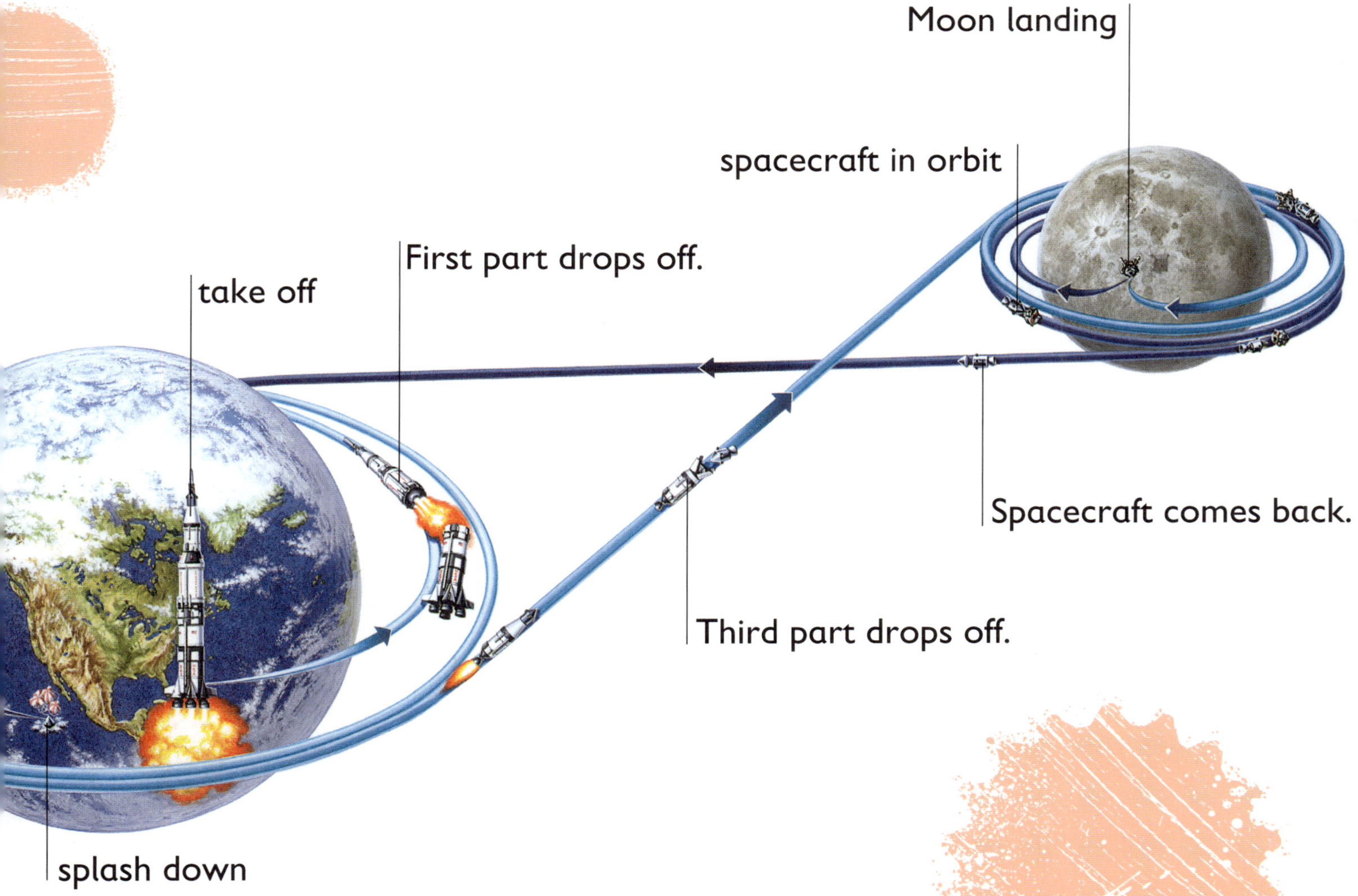

Moon landing

spacecraft in orbit

First part drops off.

take off

Spacecraft comes back.

Third part drops off.

splash down

Up High

What do you know about mountains? Read this information about them. You'll discover more about the world around you. Try the word puzzles, too.

It is cold at the top of the highest mountains. Few animals live there. Only low plants can grow. Lower down, on the slopes, where the weather is milder, many plants and animals can survive. The Himalayas, in Asia, are the world's highest mountains. Nothing lives on the peaks, but forests lower down are home to many kinds of birds. Mount Everest is the world's highest mountain on land. But there are even higher mountains under the sea.

1 Look closely at the pictures. What is my name? Write your answers in the spaces below.

(a) I am a mountain in Japan. ....

(b) I am a mountain bird with white spots. ....

(c) I am a mountain in France. ....

(d) I am a mountain in Nepal. ....

Mount Everest, Nepal

Mont Blanc, France

Mount Fuji, Japan

2   How many words of three letters can you find in
    the word 'mountains'?

    8 words = Good   12 words = Very Good   15 words = Excellent

    ....

    ....

    ....

    ....

    ....

3   Read the story carefully and look at the pictures.
    Are these sentences True (T) or False (F), or is there
    Not Enough Information (NEI) for you to decide?
    Colour in the star next to the correct answer.

    (a) Mount Fuji is a snow-capped mountain.   ☆ T   ☆ F   ☆ NEI
    (b) The Himalayas are in France.   ☆ T   ☆ F   ☆ NEI
    (c) Mont Blanc is under the sea.   ☆ T   ☆ F   ☆ NEI
    (d) The red-billed magpie sings loudly.   ☆ T   ☆ F   ☆ NEI
    (e) Low plants live where animals cannot.   ☆ T   ☆ F   ☆ NEI

spotted forktail
red-billed magpie

Himalayan monal

Travelling Overland

What do you know about ways of travelling overland? Have fun with the word puzzles and activities when you finish reading the story.

In earlier times, travelling long distances was difficult and often dangerous. Modern transport has changed all that. Railways and highways cross continents. Aircraft travel swiftly over land and sea. In the picture, a long train winds its way across the desert in Australia. It looks like a huge snake. The train is carrying iron ore towards the coast. From there, ships will take it to Japan.

1 Read the phrases below and make up a rhyme for each answer. Each word you choose has to be describing something you can travel in. For example:

A bus that carries awful insects? A roach coach.

Now it's your turn:

(a) A railway that carries wheat? A grain ....

(b) An automobile that carries famous people? A star ....

(c) An aircraft that carries water to farms? A rain ....

(d) A pony that carries ketchup? A sauce ....

(e) A helicopter that carries insects? A hopper ....

(f) A small ship that carries jackets? A coat ....

2 Match these sentence beginnings with the correct sentence ends. Draw lines to the correct answers.

Aircraft travel swiftly   was difficult long ago.

Travelling long distances   continents by car or truck.

Modern transport has   across the desert.

Highways help us cross   over land and sea.

Railways can carry goods   changed the way we travel.

3 Use the letters of the word 'OVERLAND' to fill in this sudoku. Each letter appears once in each line across and down, and once in each mini-grid.

	A	E	R	N		V	
	L	V					A
		D	V	L	R		
A							N
		L		D	A	O	E
				V	N		
		N		E		L	
L	V			A		D	

In what continent is this train travelling?

Mighty Meat-eater

What do you know about *Tyrannosaurus*? Read this information about it. Use a dictionary to find the meaning of new words. Try the word puzzles, too.

Many dinosaurs were huge. Others were very small. Some dinosaurs hunted for their food, and some ate nothing but plants. *Tyrannosaurus* was large and fierce. This dinosaur had strong back legs, but small arms. It had four claws on each leg and two on each arm. It lived and hunted in North America. The mouth of *Tyrannosaurus* was huge and it had long, sharp teeth. With its powerful jaws, it could crunch up the bones of animals that it caught.

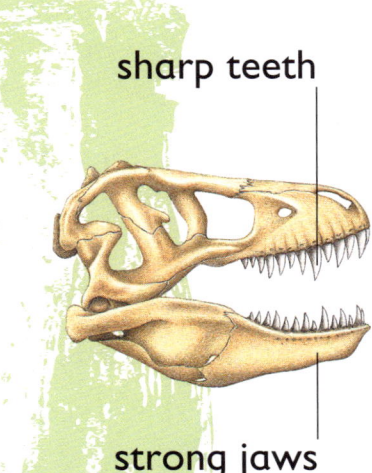

sharp teeth

strong jaws

1. Read the story carefully and then read these sentences. Are they True (T) or False (F), or is there Not Enough Information (NEI) for you to decide?
   Colour in the star next to the correct answer.

   (a) Some dinosaurs ate only plants. ☆ T ☆ F ☆ NEI

   (b) *Tyrannosaurus* ate meat and plants. ☆ T ☆ F ☆ NEI

   (c) A *Tyrannosaurus* had 16 claws. ☆ T ☆ F ☆ NEI

   (d) *Tyrannosaurus* looked fierce. ☆ T ☆ F ☆ NEI

   (e) All dinosaurs lived in North America. ☆ T ☆ F ☆ NEI

2. Unscramble these letters to make words from the story.

(a) aroundis ....

(b) harps ....

(c) mars ....

(d) flowerup ....

(e) eat ....

(f) manilas ....

(g) gels ....

3. Copy and colour the picture of *Tyrannosaurus* in the box below.

big teeth

Mummy Cases

Read the story about the cases for ancient Egyptian mummies. If you find a new word, look at the words around it to help work out the meaning.

For nearly 3,000 years Egyptians made mummies of their dead. They put them in painted coffins. Mummies were wrapped in linen sheets. Then the body was placed inside a set of cases. Each case was painted with pictures of gods. Sometimes cats were made into mummies. They were buried in special animal cemeteries near temples. They were not pets. These mummies were offerings to the gods.

cat mummy

1. Look closely at the pictures. Which is which? Write the letter next to the correct answer.

    top of inner mummy case ....

    wrapped mummy with mask ....

    top of outer mummy case ....

    bottom of outer mummy case ....

    bottom of inner mummy case ....

2. Search the story for clues for how to make these words mean more than one. Write them in the spaces below.

    (a) coffin ....

    (b) mummy ....

    (c) cemetery ....

3 Fill in the crossword with words from the story.

			¹C					
		²	A					
³			S					
	⁴		E					
	⁵		S					

Across

1. Mummies were put in painted ……………………… .
2. Each case was ……………………… with pictures of gods.
3. Egyptians made ……………………… of the dead.
4. Mummy cats were buried in animal ……………………… .
5. Mummies were wrapped in linen ……………………… .

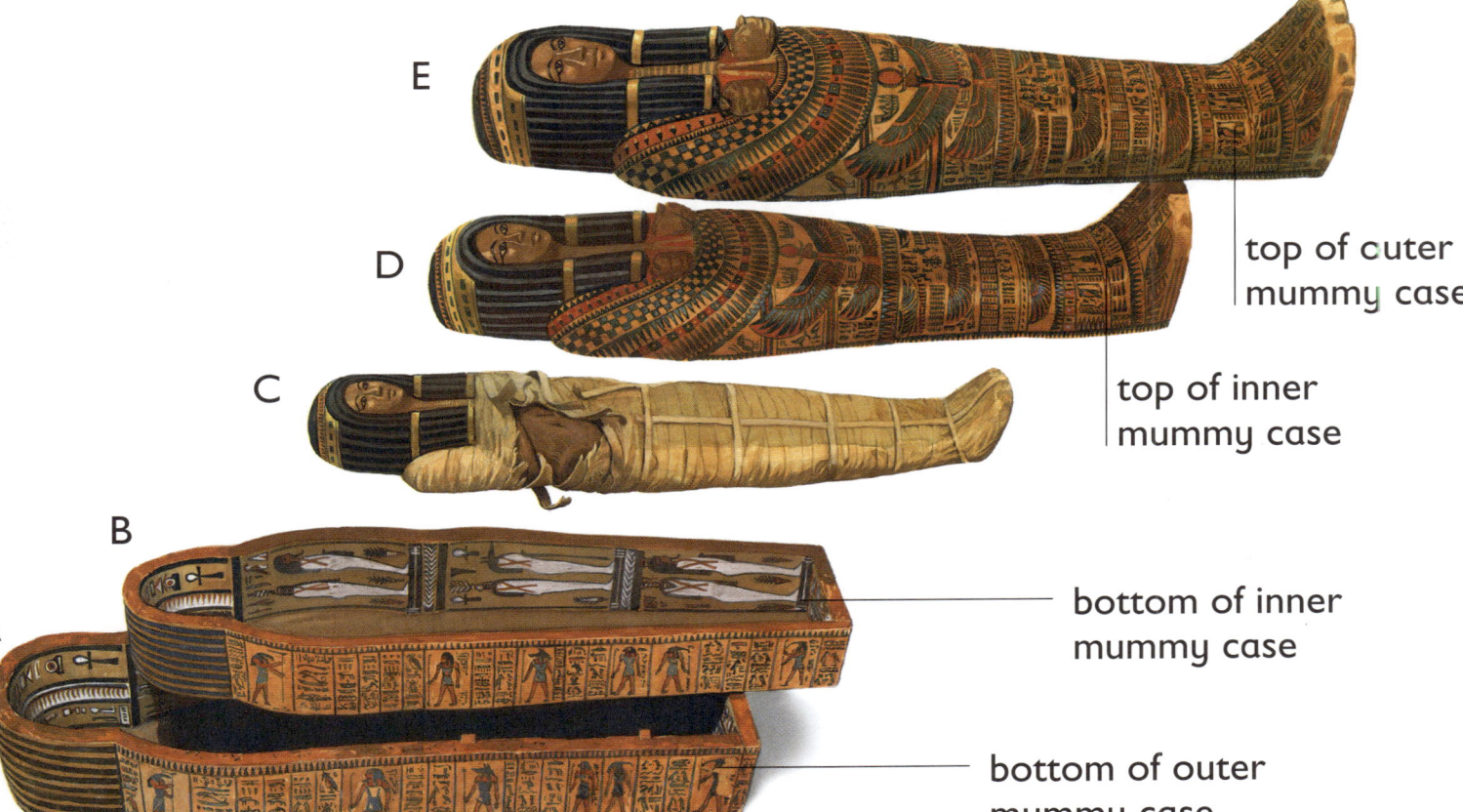

Cold Extremes

Read the information about life at the opposite ends of Earth. Use a dictionary to find the meaning of new words. Try the word puzzles, too.

Polar bears and emperor penguins live at the opposite ends of Earth. Both live where it is very cold. Emperor penguins spend all their life in Antarctica. They have feathers, but they cannot fly. They can swim fast. The male emperor penguin cares for the eggs. The female catches fish. Polar bears inhabit northern Arctic regions. A polar bear's thick white fur protects it against the cold. Fish and seals are these bears' favourite food.

emperor penguins

1 Which is which? Colour the stars that fit the description.

	polar bear	emperor penguin
(a) eats fish	☆	☆
(b) has a bill	☆	☆
(c) eats pancakes	☆	☆
(d) has fur	☆	☆
(e) has feathers	☆	☆
(f) lives near the North Pole (Arctic)	☆	☆
(g) lives near the South Pole (Antarctic)	☆	☆
(h) lives in a cold place	☆	☆
(i) eats seals	☆	☆

2 Unscramble these letters to make words from the story.

(a) alpor basre .... (animals)

(b) hatEr .... (a place)

(c) clod .... (a feeling)

(d) pinegun .... (an animal)

(e) sales .... (animals)

(f) catAractin .... (a place)

3 Can you help the polar bear find its way through the maze to get to its home?

polar bears

Healthy and Fit in Ancient Greece

Let's find out about health and fitness in ancient Greece. Complete the activities when you finish reading the story.

Keeping fit was important to the Greeks. People went to the gymnasium to exercise and do sports. The Olympic Games began at Olympia, in Greece. They lasted for five days. Only men competed in these games. In the picture on this page, a sportsman is throwing a discus. To cure diseases and injury, Greek doctors often used medicines they made from herbs. Doctors thought that if a sick person was made to bleed, the illness would leave the body.

discus throwing at the Olympics

1 Answer these questions about the story.

(a) How did the Greeks keep fit?

....

(b) What modern sports festival began with the Greeks?

....

(c) How long did that festival last and who could compete?

....

(d) What sort of medicines did Ancient Greeks often use?

....

(e) Why did doctors make people bleed?

....

2 Write down the first letter and then write every second letter after that. Go around twice. The secret message will tell you why ancient Greek doctors used the herb called motherwort.

The secret message is:

....

....

....

Start >>	D	r	o	w	c	o	t	r
e								o
n								t
h								r
i								t
t								s
a								o
o								u
p	m	e	d	s	e	a	s	e

3 Which words in the story mean the opposite of these words and phrases? Write your answers in the spaces below.

(a) ended ....

(b) hardly ever ....

(c) make worse ....

(d) unfit ....

doctor taking blood

Bicycles and Tyres

Read about the invention of bicycles and tyres. If you find a new word, look at the words around it to help work out the meaning.

The wheel may be the greatest invention ever made. Without wheels, our world and our lives would be very different. Bicycles use wheels to move. They are now the main kind of transport for many people. On the first bicycles, called dandy horses, riders pushed themselves along with their feet. When pedals were invented, in about **1840**, bicycle riding became much easier. In **1887**, John Dunlop invented air-filled tyres for his son's bike. Before then, tyres were made of solid rubber.

mountain bike

1. Use the pictures to help you number these sentences in the correct order.

    .... Two people could ride the same bike.

    .... People rode bikes with wheels of different sizes.

    .... People rode bikes called dandy horses.

    .... The modern racing bike was invented.

    .... Women in long skirts could ride bikes safely.

1790 dandy horse

1870 penny-farthing

1879 safety bike

2. Do these pairs of sentences have the Same (S) meaning or a Different (D) meaning? Colour in the star next to the correct answer.

   (a) (i) For many people, bicycles are now the main kind of transport.
       (ii) Now, the main kind of transport is bicycles. ☆ S ☆ D

   (b) (i) In about 1840, when pedals were invented, bicycle riding became easier.
       (ii) Bicycle riding became easier in about 1840. ☆ S ☆ D

   (c) (i) The wheel may be the greatest invention ever made.
       (ii) The greatest invention ever made is the wheel. ☆ S ☆ D

   (d) (i) The tandem bicycle has two seats and four pedals.
       (ii) The tandem bicycle is built for two people. ☆ S ☆ D

3. Which bicycle am I? Write the correct answers in the spaces provided.

   (a) You push yourself along with your feet to move me. ....
   (b) I am built for speed. ....
   (c) My wheels are different sizes. ....
   (d) I am a bicycle built for two. ....
   (e) I was invented with safety in mind. ....

1980s tandem bike

1990s racing bike

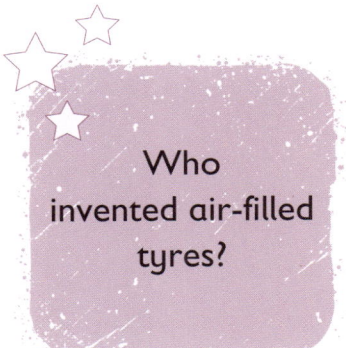

Who invented air-filled tyres?

Strong Swimmers

Let's find out about animals that live in icy Antarctica. Complete the fun activities when you finish reading the story.

Ice and snow always cover the ground in Earth's polar regions. Antarctica, around the South Pole, is the coldest place on Earth. Many penguins live there. These birds cannot fly, but they swim very strongly. Their thick feathers help protect them from the cold. Most birds flap their wings as they fly through the air. Penguins flap their wings as they swim. They need to swim fast to escape from seals and some whales that hunt them.

1. Finish each sentence by circling the correct word.

    (a) The ..South / North.. Pole is the coldest place on Earth.

    (b) Penguins ..cannot / can.. swim strongly.

    (c) Ice and ..trees / snow.. cover the ground in polar regions.

    (d) Penguins ..cannot / can.. fly through the air.

    (e) Seals are ..hungry / thirsty.. for penguins.

2. Match the jigsaw parts to make sentences. Use different colours to match the sentence parts.

Penguins flap — their wings — as they swim.

The South Pole — is in — Antarctica.

Thick feathers — protect penguins — from the cold.

Seals and whales — hunt — penguins for food.

3. Look at the picture. Can you imagine what they might be saying? Write your answers in the speech bubbles.

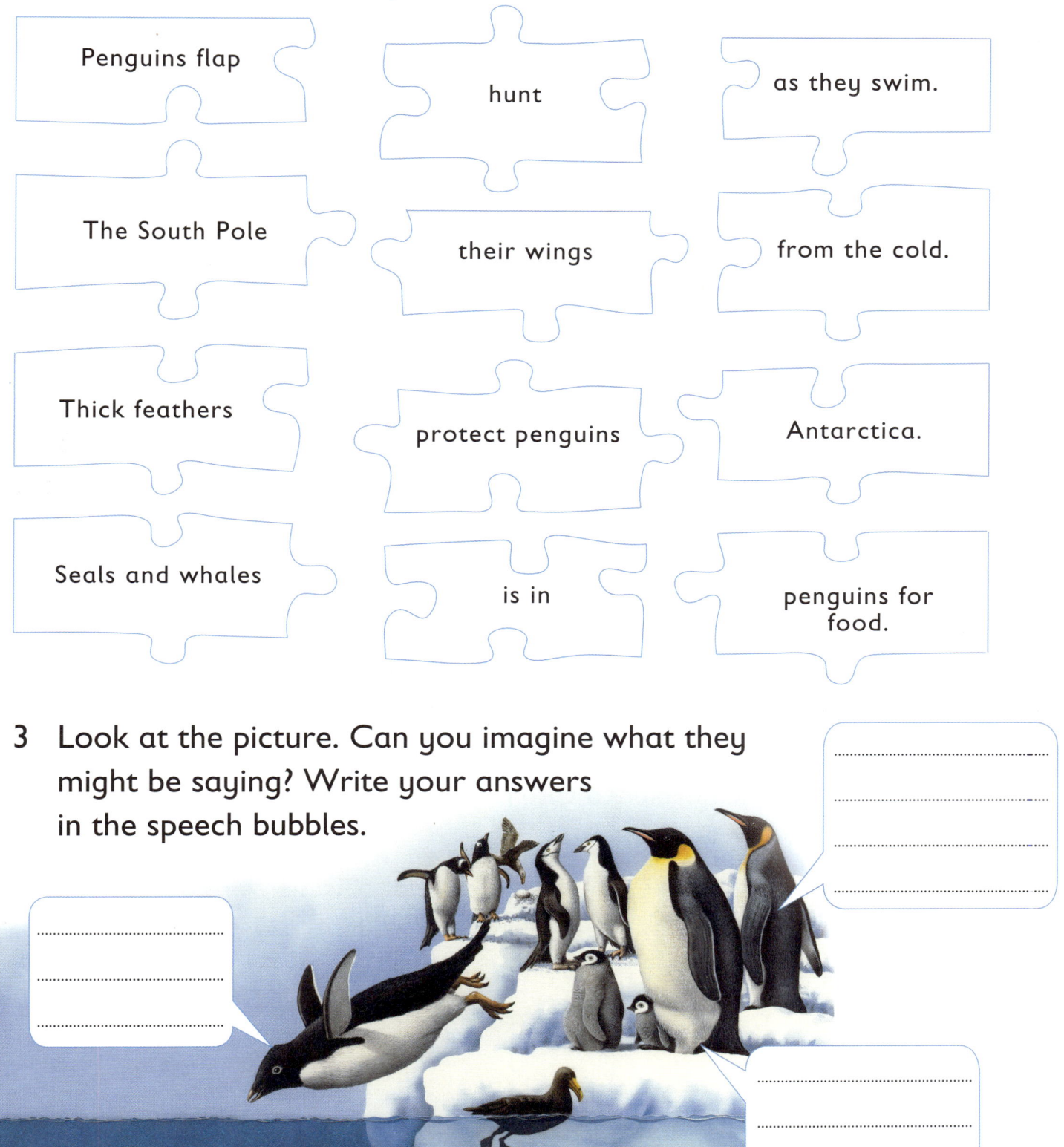

Forbidden City

What do you know about the Forbidden City in Beijing, China? Read this information about it. Use a dictionary to find the meaning of new words. Try the word puzzles, too.

Many great buildings in the world are small, simple constructions. Others are grand and impressive. In Beijing, China, stands a huge group of timber palaces. Together they are called the Forbidden City. Only the emperor and officials were allowed to go there. In the picture, the emperor is being carried towards his throne in the Hall of Supreme Harmony. The Forbidden City is now a public museum. Visitors can see paintings, statues and other things of interest from the past.

1 Write your own questions to match these answers.

   (a) Question: ....
       Answer: The Forbidden City is found in China.

   (b) Question: ....
       Answer: Only the emperor and special officials were allowed to go there.

   (c) Question: ....
       Answer: The palaces of the Forbidden City are made from timber.

2 Which words in the story mean the same as these words?
   Write your answers in the spaces below.

   (a) a ruler ....

   (b) grand and impressive buildings ....

   (c) a special chair that a ruler sits on ....

3 You can play this 'Forbidden Number' game on your own or with a friend. The aim is to try to reach 100 without making a mistake. The forbidden number is 4. Take it in turns to count forwards from one. When a number is reached that has the 'forbidden number' in it (e.g. 4, 14, 24) or can be divided by 4 (e.g. 8, 12, 16), say 'BUZZ' instead.

   If you make a mistake – go back to the start! For a variation, choose a different forbidden number between 2 and 9.

Comets in Orbit

Learn about comets in space. Then complete the fun activities. They will help you discover more about the world around you.

Comets are balls of dirty ice in space. Like planets, they move around the Sun. When a comet nears the Sun, its centre, or nucleus, warms up. It produces a cloud of dust and gas, which we call a coma. If you see a comet in the sky, you'll notice its long tail. This streak of dust and gas can be millions of kilometres long. A famous comet is called Halley's comet, which comes around every 76 years.

1. Find the opposites of these words and phrases in the story.
   - (a) clean ice
   - (b) cools down
   - (c) short tail
   - (d) outside

2. Halley's comet was last seen in 1986. In what year will it be seen again?

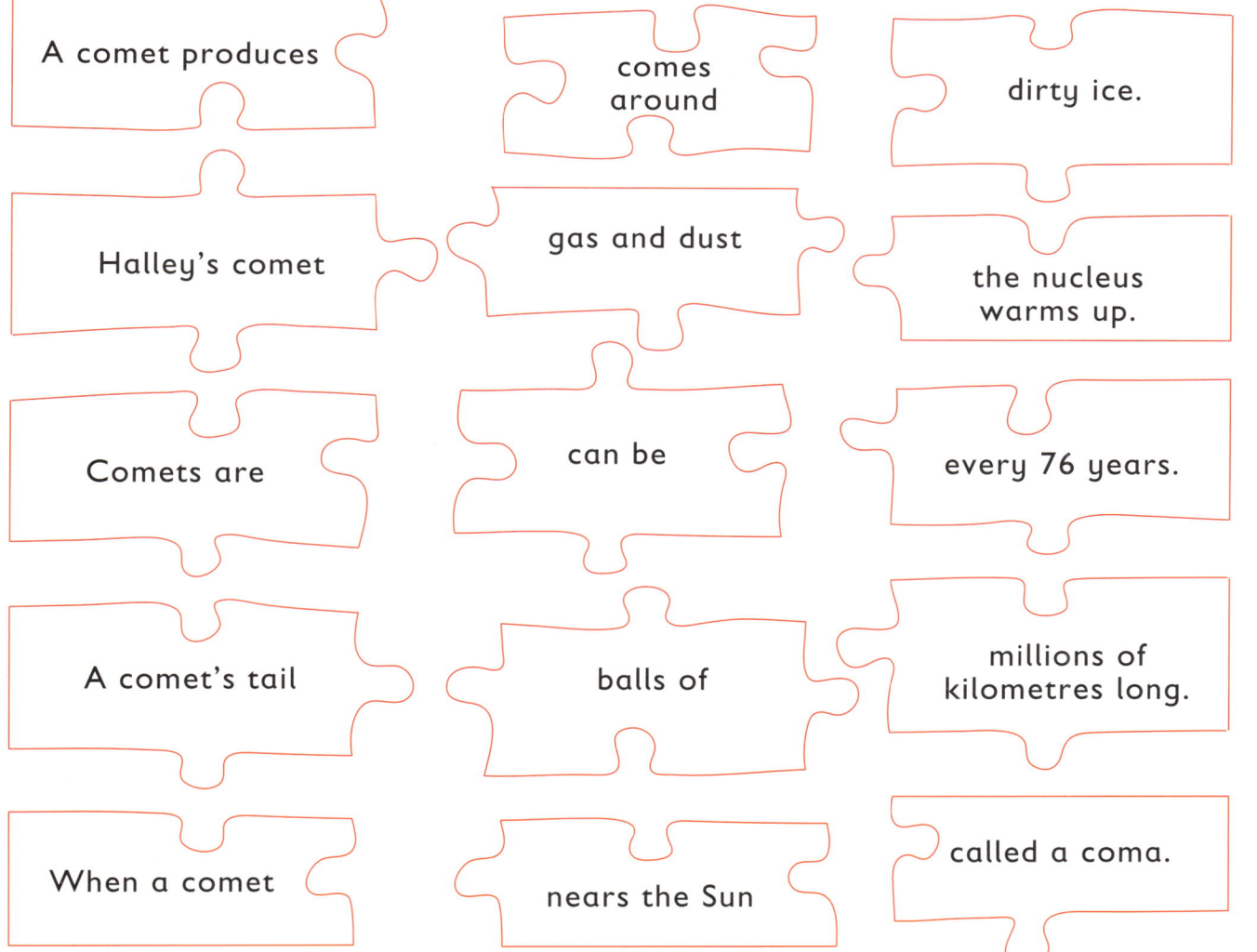

3 Match the jigsaw parts to make sentences. Use different colours to match the sentence parts.

- A comet produces | gas and dust | dirty ice.
- Halley's comet | comes around | every 76 years.
- Comets are | balls of | dirty ice.
- A comet's tail | can be | millions of kilometres long.
- When a comet | nears the Sun | the nucleus warms up.

(Jigsaw pieces: A comet produces / Halley's comet / Comets are / A comet's tail / When a comet — comes around / gas and dust / can be / balls of / nears the Sun — dirty ice. / the nucleus warms up. / every 76 years. / millions of kilometres long. / called a coma.)

Cleaner Shrimps

Read the story about how shrimps help fish. If you find a new word, look at the words around it to help work out the meaning.

Tiny animals live on the body of some fish and sharks. We call them parasites. Some shrimps eat parasites on fish. A colourful shrimp that cleans fish is the coral banded shrimp. Cleaner shrimps live on coral reefs. They often work in groups as they clean parasites from fish. They even go into the mouths of some fish. In the picture on this page, you can see the crown of thorns starfish. Unlike the shrimp, it feeds on coral and damages the reef.

crown of thorns starfish

1. Colour in the star next to the word that is the odd one out. Then say why you have chosen this word.

   (a) ☆ fish   ☆ bird   ☆ shark   ☆ shrimp

   Why? ....

   (b) ☆ umbrella   ☆ raincoat   ☆ sunglasses   ☆ gumboots

   Why? ....

   (c) ☆ chess   ☆ tennis   ☆ football   ☆ baseball

   Why? ....

   (d) ☆ banana   ☆ apple   ☆ orange   ☆ cabbage

   Why? ....

2 Finish each sentence by circling the correct word.

(a) Coral shrimps often ..clean / chase.. parasites from a fish's body.

(b) The ..crown / circle.. of thorns starfish damages coral reefs.

(c) Parasites ..love / live.. on some fish and sharks.

(d) Sometimes cleaner shrimps go into the ..moths / mouths.. of a fish.

3 You can play this game with a friend. You both start at the same time. Use the Start Letter and see if you can think of four animals that start with that letter. You score 10 points for each word, but only 5 points if you both get the same word. You score 0 points for the wrong spelling.

Start Letter					Score
L					
G					
B					
S					
T					
C					

The first person to complete the row calls out 'Stop'!

coral banded shrimp

shrimp

A Pharaoh's Funeral

Here is some information about a pharaoh's funeral in ancient Egypt. Read the story. Then enjoy completing the activities.

Pharaohs were rulers in ancient Egypt. At the funeral of a pharaoh, the mummy, in its coffins, was placed on a large sleigh. When the sleigh reached the River Nile, it was pulled onto a barge that took it to the other side of the river. Then it was pulled across the desert to a tomb. Some tombs were cut deep into desert cliffs. Robbers often broke into tombs. That is why pharaohs' tombs were built in hidden places.

1 Do these pairs of sentences have the Same (S) meaning or a Different (D) meaning?
   Colour in the star next to the correct answer.

   (a) (i) Pharaohs were the rulers of ancient Egypt.
       (ii) Long ago, the rulers of Egypt were pharaohs. ☆ S ☆ D

   (b) (i) At the funeral of a pharaoh, the mummy was placed in a coffin.
       (ii) At the funeral, a pharaoh was buried with its mummy in a coffin.

   (c) (i) Robbers often broke into the tombs of pharaohs.
       (ii) Pharaohs' tombs were frequently robbed.

2 Answer these questions about the story.

(a) Who were the pharaohs?

....

(b) What moved the pharaoh's mummy and its coffin around land?

....

(c) Why were pharaohs buried in hidden places?

....

3 In this word puzzle, write down the first letter and then write every second letter after that. Go around twice. The secret message will tell you where a pharaoh could be buried.

								a								
							d		l							
						m				r						
					b						u					
				i								y				
			e										o			
		d												p		
	b														c	
Start >>	A	u	p	r	h	i	a	e	r	d	a	i	o	n	h	a

The secret message is:

....

....

Long and Sticky

Learn about how chameleons change colour. Complete the fun activities when you finish reading the story.

Chameleons are lizards with a long tongue. Their tail and toes can curl around branches. They can change colour when they need to hide from an enemy. A chameleon's tongue is as long as its whole body. The sticky end of the tongue traps insects and other small animals. Most chameleons eat insects. Some also eat birds. There are many kinds of chameleons. Most of them live in forests in Africa and on the island of Madagascar.

1. Read these sentences about the story. Do you Agree (A) or Disagree (D)?
   Colour in the star next to the correct answer.

   (a) The chameleon has a short tongue. ☆ A ☆ D

   (b) Some chameleons live in Africa. ☆ A ☆ D

   (c) Camouflage helps the chameleon hide from an enemy. ☆ A ☆ D

   (d) Birds can be prey for some chameleons. ☆ A ☆ D

   (e) Look at the picture on page 131. The chameleon's tail helps it stay steady. ☆ A ☆ D

   (f) The end of the chameleon's tongue has thorns. ☆ A ☆ D

The sticky end traps insects.

toe

curly tail

2. The chameleon changes colour when it hides. What colour would be best for an animal hiding in these places? Choose your answers from the words in the group below.

| black | white | yellow | light green |
| dark green | blue | brown | red | grey |

(a) a thick, dark forest   ....

(b) a sandy shore   ....

(c) a snowy mountain   ....

(d) a grassy hill   ....

(e) a muddy puddle   ....

3. What am I?

My first letter is in 'rule' but not in 'rue'.
My second letter is not in 'bull' but is in 'bill'.
My third letter is in 'buzz' but not in 'bun'.
My fourth letter is not in 'cell' but is in 'call'.
My fifth letter is in 'brat' but not in 'tab'.
My sixth letter is in 'lady' but not in 'lay'.

I am a   ....

Join the Dots

Join the dots to see the Egyptian queen's crown.

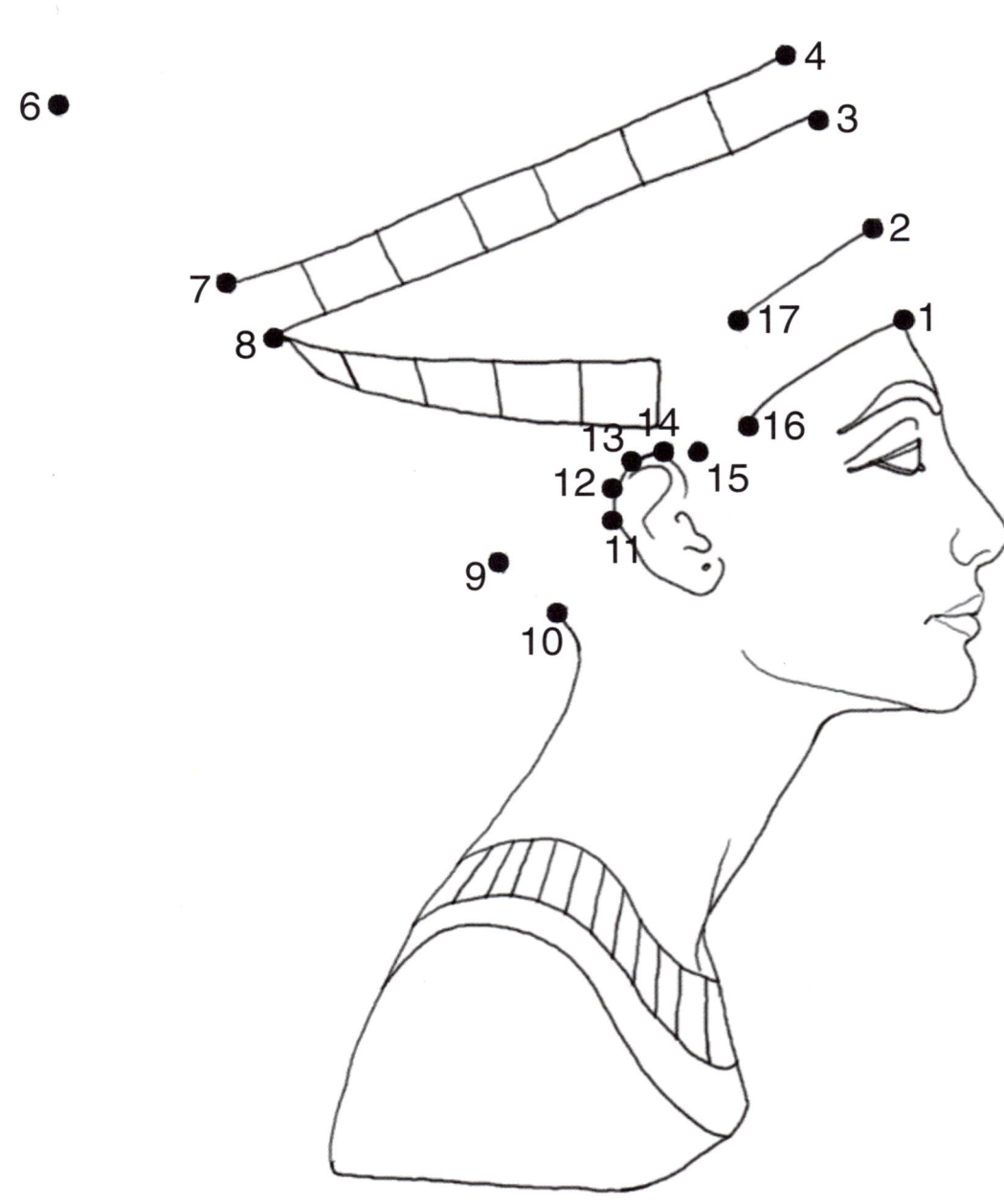

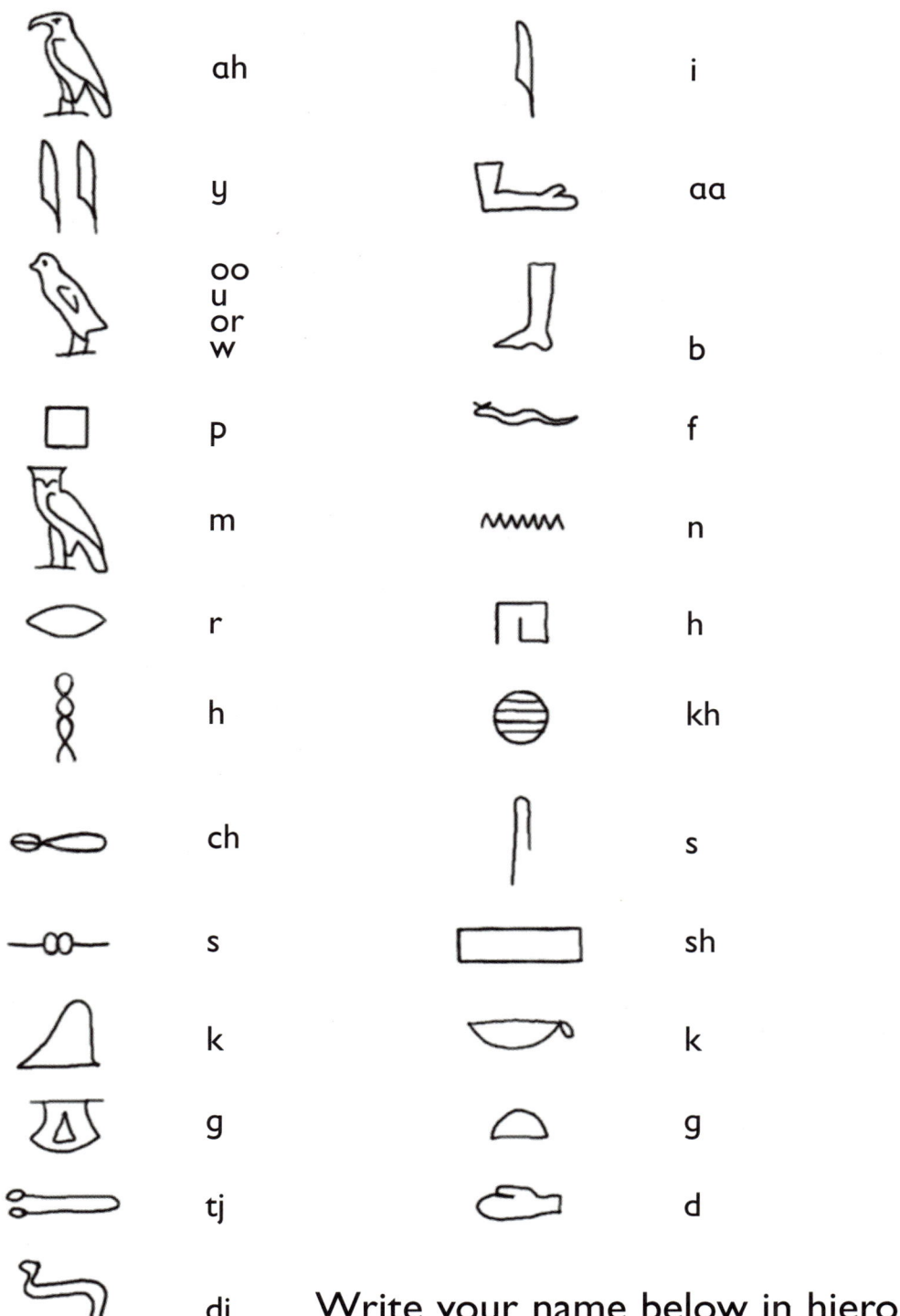

Write your name below in hieroglyphs.

_____

Answers

Answers

Solutions to crosswords, sudokus and other puzzles from pages 4–67 are on pages 138–139.

4–5
1. (a) T (b) NEI (c) NEI (d) NEI (e) T
2. (a) nose (b) mouth
3. Crocodiles do not have to work hard to find food. They lie still in the water waiting until an animal comes near. Then they grab their victim in their strong jaws.

6–7
1. (a) a ruler (b) two people (c) northern India
2. (a) True (b) False (c) True
3. Crossword
4. Mahal

Star box: 14

8–9
1. (a) T (b) T (c) NEI (d) T (e) F (f) F (g) NEI
2. (a) Osiris and Horus (b) Anubis, Isis and Horus
   (c) Anubis and Horus (d) Horus
   (e) Osiris (f) Anubis, Isis and Horu

10–11
1. (a) S (b) D
2. The tropics are a hot, wet part of Earth's surface.
   In cold climates most plants stay close to the ground.
   In deserts only a few plants grow.
   In warm climates leafy trees and grasses grow.
   Trees and plants grow easily in warm, wet areas.
3. region, climates, deserts, surface

12–13
1. Crossword
2. corals
3. (a) hard (b) soft (c) tiny (d) gives (e) many (f) build up
4. (a) T (b) NEI (c) NEI (d) T

Star box: yes

14–15
1. (a) Italy
   (b) It was buried by a volcano.
   (c) No, because they didn't know Mount Vesuvius was a volcano.
2. 2 Mount Vesuvius erupts.
   5 Pompeii is rediscovered.
   1 The people of Pompeii do not know that Mount Vesuvius is a volcano.
   4 Pompeii is forgotten.
   3 Pompeii is buried under hot ash and rock.
3. (a) the donkey is frightened (b) hot rocks are falling

Star box: It is erupting.

16–17
1. (a) F (b) T (c) NEI (d) F (e) NEI (f) T
2. (a) birds that fly (b) to stay still in the air
   (c) a sugary drink (d) to drift

18–19
1. The world's highest mountain, Mount Everest, is in the Himalayas.
   In some parts of the world, mountains rise high into the air.
   The Matterhorn is a high mountain between Switzerland and Italy.
   Near the top of some mountains it is always cold.
2. (a) T (b) F (c) T
   (d) F (e) NEI (f) T
3. (a) range (b) string (c) library (d) fleet

20–21
1. (a) a slave (b) They captured them in wars
   (c) slaves and labourers (d) to work for money to live
   (e) by paying money
2. (a) Fact (b) Opinion (c) Opinion (d) Fact (e) Opinion
3. My feet are all purple now. B
   Look! Can you get those big grapes? F
   My music will keep us happy. H
   I feel like a bird up here. E
   In go the grapes! A
   This basket gets heavier with each trip. C

22–23
1. (a) camel, squirrel, gerenuk
   (b) It stores fat and moisture in the humps on its back.
   (c) It stores nuts and seeds in hollow trees.
   (d) It gets moisture from leaves.
2. (a) nuts (b) animals (c) desert (d) never
   (e) leaves (f) need (g) trees (h) later
3. (a) camel and gerenuk (b) squirrel
   (c) camel and gerenuk (d) camel
   (e) squirrel (f) gerenuk (g) squirrel

24–25
1. (a) Earth (b) solar system (c) universe (d) Earth
2. Crossword

26–27
1. (a) Neil Armstrong (b) 12
   (c) Gravity is a force that pulls things towards the centre of a planet or moon. (d) It would float around.
2. (a) space + craft (b) foot + prints (c) splash + down
   (e) every + thing (f) man + kind
3. Apollo   giant   gravity
   golf   walked   moon

Star box: the United States of America

28–29
1. (a) chameleon (b) Australian shingleback (c) leaf-tailed gecko (d) collared lizard (e) skink
2. (a) because it senses danger
   (b) It lifts its tail in the air and runs on its back legs.
   (c) A new tail grows.
3. Crossword

30–31
1. (a) for fun (b) by computers (c) because they are strapped in
2. Word ladders

32–33
1. (a) to stop it from rotting (b) Anubis (c) a priest
2. (a) True (b) False (c) True
3. 3 Wrap the body in bandages.
   1 Remove the lungs, liver and brains.
   4 Put the body in a coffin.
   2 Dry the body out.
4. (a) stop (b) lungs (c) last

34–35
1. (a) in a hole, or burrow, under the ground
   (b) silk (c) by mixing earth with silk
3. Sudoku

36–37
1. (a) Africa (b) Earth (c) Moon
   (d) No, because Earth was covered with hot, melted rock.
2. (a) rock in space (b) thrown (c) slowly
3. 3 Broken rocks were flung into space.
   2 An asteroid hit Earth.
   1 Earth was formed.
   5 Broken rocks joined together to make the Moon.
   4 Broken rocks formed a ring around Earth.

38–39
1. (a) these cold parts of the world (b) Great auks
   (c) hunted them for food and used them for bait
   (d) the weather got warmer (e) great auk, mammoth
2. (a) neither (b) great auk (c) mammoth
   (d) mammoth (e) mammoth and great auk
3. Maze

40–41
1. Long ago, dinosaurs made nests and laid eggs just like birds do today. Baby dinosaurs hatched from these eggs. Mother dinosaur fed her baby dinosaurs. She looked after them until they could walk.
2. (a) D (b) A (c) A (d) A (e) D (f) D (g) A (h) D
3. Lunch is ready. C   That looks yum, Mum! A
   Help! B

42–43
1. (a) were delivered to homes (b) to cool food
   (c) from the cistern to the bowl (d) 60 years ago
   (e) the S-bend of the toilet
3. Word search

44–45
1. (a) C (b) A (c) B
2. (a) T (b) F (c) F (d) NEI (e) NEI
3. Word ladder

46–47
1. (a) clownfish (b) jellyfish (c) shark and clownfish
   (d) shark (e) octopus
   (f) shark, jellyfish, sponge, clownfish and octopus
2. Word search

48–49
1. (a) T (b) NEI (c) F (d) F (e) T (f) NEI
2. (a) suck up (b) huge, giant, large (c) upwards
   (d) over (e) large number
3. cloud

50–51
1. (a) up, down, forwards, backwards
   (b) rotors
   (c) It can reach places that an aeroplane cannot reach.
   (e) hover
2. chopper
3. (a) down (b) float (c) fast (d) places (e) control

52–53
1. roof colour brown
   extra column in archway on left
   extra roof spire on left of building
   windows missing under second dome from left
   gold dome missing from central tower
   colour changed on dome on right
   roof spire missing on right of building
2. Crossword
3. Basil

54–55
1. (a) S (b) D (c) D (d) D (e) D (f) D
2. Word Ladders
3. (a) poor (b) modern (c) blunt

Answers continued...

56–57
1. (a) a large horn (b) in cold regions near the North Pole
   (c) winter (d) Its toes spread out to give a better grip.
2. Reindeer have long horns called antlers. In winter the antlers fall off. In spring the antlers begin to grow. In summer, skin covers the antlers until they drop off again in winter. Reindeer live near the North Pole in very cold regions.

58–59
1. (a) group of stars (b) cooler part of the Sun
   (c) centre (d) outside part of the Sun
2. (a) Sun and Moon (b) knife and fork
   (c) bread and butter (d) silver and gold
   (e) salt and pepper (f) table and chair
   (g) cup and saucer (h) cat and dog
3. The Milky Way is the name of a galaxy. Our Sun is part of that galaxy. It is also the centre of our solar system. Life on Earth gets both light (heat) and heat (light) from the Sun. The outside edge of the Sun is the corona. The centre of the Sun is the core.

60–61
1. Possible questions are:
   (a) What did *Stegosaurus* use its spikes for?
   (b) How did *Stegosaurus* get its food?
   (c) How long ago did the dinosaurs die out?
   (d) How did the bony plates on *Stegosaurus* help it?
   (e) How would you feel if you met *Stegosaurus*?
2. (a) walrus (b) eggbeater
3. Maze

62–63
1. (a) the Curia (b) once each year (c) an emperor
2. senator missing
   colour of stripe on Lucius's toga changed
   wreath on Lucius's head
   wreath missing from Titus's head
   white-haired senator has brown hair
   senator next to him has red stripe
   scroll missing from the messenger's hands
   the braid on Titus's toga is missing

64–65
1. (a) It struck an iceberg. (b) It was too dark.
   (c) 1985 (d) 706
2. Maze
Star box: an iceberg

66–67
1. (a) F (b) F (c) NEI (d) T (e) T (f) NEI
2. 3 The hull breaks apart.
   1 The water enters the bow and holes for the anchor.
   4 The ship finally sinks.
   2 The *Titanic* is sinking bow first. A funnel is lost.
3. Crossword

6–7
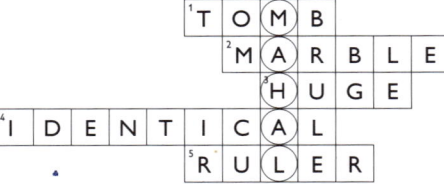

12–13

24–25
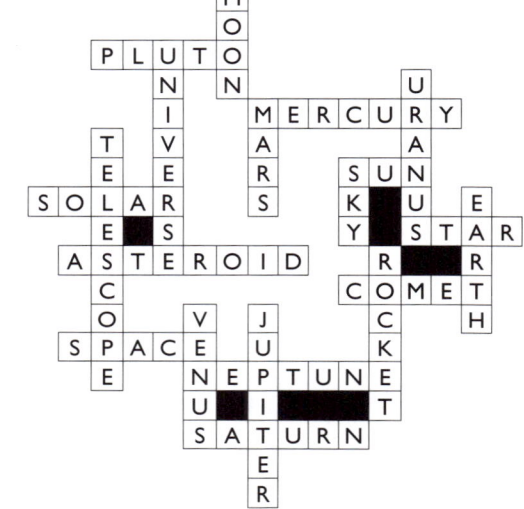

28–29

30–31
c	a	r		r	o	l	l
f	a	r		r	o	l	e
f	u	r		r	o	d	e
f	u	n		r	i	d	e

34–35

R	D	S	E	P	I
P	I	E	S	D	R
I	S	P	D	R	E
D	E	R	I	S	P
S	P	I	R	E	D
E	R	D	P	I	S

38–39

42–43

44–45

f	i	v	e
d	i	v	e
d	o	v	e

46–47

52–53

¹BUILDINGS
²RUSSIA
³SNOW
⁴ONIONS
⁵CATHEDRAL

54–55

p	e	n
p	a	n
p	a	l

k	i	t
b	i	t
b	a	t
b	a	g

60–61

64–65

66–67

¹SOUTHAMPTON
²UNSINKABLE
³THREE
⁴MAIDEN
⁵ANCHOR
⁶LIFEBOATS
⁷ICEBERG

Answers continued...

Solutions to crosswords, sudokus and other puzzles from pages 68–131 are on pages 142–143.

68–69
1. (a) T (b) T (c) F (d) T (e) NEI
2. Crossword

70–71
1. (a) hissing, using a coloured tongue, making itself look bigger
   (b) hisses and puffs out the frill behind its neck
   (c) shows its blue tongue   (d) two
2. group, scaring, loud, tongue, frill, its
3. reptiles
4. (a) spider. Because a lizard and snake are both reptiles.
   (b) frill. Because blue and red are both colours.
   (c) safety. Because danger and risk have the same meaning.

72–73
1. (a) western Italy   (b) rich people
   (c) they had slaves to do all the work
2. 3 Remove peacock from oven.
   1 Put peacock in the oven.
   4 Place three small live birds inside cooked peacock.
   6 Watch the little birds fly out.
   5 Take peacock to the table and carve.
   2 Roast peacock for 1 hour.

Star box: in the picture on the back right wall

74–75
1. (a) Water drips out. Because there was a hole in the pot.
   (b) Water filled up the pot.
   (c) They showed how much water had dripped in, and how many hours had passed.
   (d) where the Sun was in the sky
2. (a) F (b) NEI (c) T (d) F (e) NEI
3. When do clocks die? — When their time is up.
   What kind of clock is crazy? — A cuckoo clock.
   How does a witch tell the time? — With a witch watch.
   What flies without wings? — Time.
   What animal keeps the time? — A watchdog.

76–77
1. (a) to fight each other in the air, to drop bombs on enemy positions
   (b) to help the aircraft to fly faster (c) It has a strange shape.
   (d) to transport people, to transport goods
   (e) It can pick up the speed and position of things like planes.
2. Word search

78–79
1. (a) F (b) T (c) NEI (d) NEI (e) NEI
2. Beavers can build a lodge in the middle of a pond. Here they are safe from bears and wolves.
3. (a) pool   (b) home   (c) go in

Star box: to get wood to help build a lodge

80–81
1. On a clear night, you can see thousands of stars. They are part of the Milky Way. It is easier to see more stars if it is dark. Bright city lights can block out the view. One of the brightest lights is the planet Venus. People who study stars and planets use a radio telescope with a large dish to pick up signals from space.
2. an astronomer studies the stars

82–83
1. (a) hard   (b) buried   (c) cuts   (d) drift
2. (a) Question: What is an iceberg?
      Answer: It is a floating piece of glacier.
   (b) Question: Why is it hard to know the size of an iceberg?
      Answer: Because most of an iceberg is hidden.
   (c) Question: What is a glacier?
      Answer: It is a solid river of ice.
   (d) Question: Where would you find an iceberg?
      Answer: In cold seas near a glacier.

84–85
1. Possible questions include:
   (a) When was the Sydney Opera House built?
   (b) What materials were used to build the Sydney Opera House?
   (c) What do the shells of the Sydney Opera House look a lot like?
2. (a) many   (b) impressive   (c) new   (d) slowly
   (e) white   (f) large
3. Crossword

86–87
1. (a) T (b) F (c) NEI (d) T (e) F (f) NEI
2. (a) Possible answers include: A woman is weaving cloth. A woman is sewing. A woman is playing with a baby.
   (b) Possible answers include: Men are talking. Men are eating. Men are lying and sitting on couches.
   (c) Possible answers include: A woman is lifting a jug. A woman is carrying a jug.
   (d) A woman is making a bed
   (e) Possible answers include: Children are playing. A girl is playing with a doll. A woman is watching the children.
   (f) Possible answers include: A woman is having a bath. A woman is washing a child.

88–89
1. (a) seagrass (b) because it blends in with seaweed and seagrass
   (c) It sucks it in through its long mouth. (d) on the male's tail
2. (a) stonefish   (b) clownfish   (c) seagrass   (d) jellyfish
3. Word search

90–91
1. (a) wind, sea   (b) Huge waves beat against the land   (c) arch
2. 3 Finally an arch loses its top to become a sea stack.
   1 As the sea wears away a cliff, caves form.
   2 Slowly, caves turn into arches.
3. earthquakes, rivers, humans, glaciers, volcanoes, fire, hurricanes
4. Word ladder

92–93
1. (a) There are plans to set up a Moon base there.
   (b) from ice at the Moon's south pole (c) from solar panels
2. (a) of the Sun (b) of the Moon (c) a station

Star box: a solar panel

94–95
1. (a) that a meteorite hit Earth and blocked out the Sun
   (b) that the climate got too hot for the dinosaurs to live
   (c) a large piece of rock or metal that comes from outer space
2. (a) S (b) D (c) D (d) S

96–97
1. (a) Opinion (b) Fact (c) Fact (d) Opinion (e) Fact
2. Crossword
3. trout

98–99
1. (a) T (b) NEI (c) T (d) F
2. Possible answers include:
   There are cracks in the wall.
   The fountain has stopped flowing.
   Tiles have fallen off the roof.
3. (a) always (b) crack (c) flood (d) uneasy

100–101
1. (a) in northern Alaska and Canada
   (b) Inuit used the skin and fur of seals and deer.
   (c) Possible answers include:
       Snowmobiles are faster and stronger than dogs.
       Snowmobiles take up less room.
       There's no need to feed or look after snowmobiles.
2. gloves, fur jacket, snow boots, straight hair, warm trousers, fur hood
3. (a) Fact (b) Opinion (c) Opinion (d) Fact (e) Opinion

Star box: eat it

102–103
1. (a) 14 (b) 4 (c) 18
2. (a) Survivors (b) Icebergs
3. Evacuation, Survivors
4. the discovery of the wreck of the *Titanic*
5. The Collision
6. 13 chapters
7. Quiz, Glossary, Index

104–105
1. 6 Spacecraft starts to return.
   1 Blast off!
   5 Lunar module lands on the Moon.
   2 First part drops off.
   7 Splash down!
   4 Spacecraft arrives at the Moon.
   3 Second and third parts drop off.
2. Maze

106–107
1. (a) Mount Fuji (b) spotted forktail (c) Mont Blanc
   (d) Mount Everest
2. Possible answers include:
   aim, ant, inn, its, man, mat, nan, nit, not, nun, nut, oat, out, sat, sin, sit, son, sum, sun, tan, tin, ton
3. (a) T (b) F (c) F (d) NEI (e) T

108–109
1. (a) train (b) car (c) plane
   (d) horse (e) chopper (f) boat
2. Aircraft travel swiftly — over land and sea.
   Travelling long distances — was difficult long ago.
   Modern transport has — changed the way we travel.
   Highways help us cross — continents by car or truck.
   Railways carry goods — across the desert.
3. Sudoku
4. Star box: Australia

110–111
1. (a) T (b) NEI (c) F (d) T (e) NEI
2. (a) dinosaur (b) sharp (c) arms (d) powerful
   (e) ate (f) animals (g) legs

112–113
1. (a) D (b) C (c) E (d) A (e) B
2. (a) coffins (b) mummies (c) cemeteries
3. Crossword

114–115
1. (a) polar bear and emperor penguin (b) emperor penguin
   (c) neither (d) polar bear (e) emperor penguin
   (f) polar bear (g) emperor penguin
   (h) polar bear and emperor penguin (i) polar bear
2. (a) polar bears (b) Earth (c) cold (d) penguin
   (e) seals (f) Antarctica
3. Maze

116–117
1. (a) by going to the gymnasium to exercise and to do sports
   (b) the Olympic Games (c) five days, only men
   (d) medicines they made from herbs
   (e) to make the illness leave the body
2. Doctors used motherwort to ease pain.
3. (a) began (b) often (c) to cure (d) fit

Answers continued...

118–119

1. 4 Two people could ride the same bike.
   2 People rode bikes with wheels of different sizes.
   1 People rode bikes called dandy horses.
   5 The modern racing bike was invented.
   3 Women in long skirts could ride bikes safely.

2. (a) D (b) S (c) D (d) S

3. (a) dandy horse (b) racing bike (c) penny-farthing
   (d) tandem bike (e) safety bike

Star box: John Dunlop

120–121

1. (a) South (b) can (c) snow (d) cannot (e) hungry
2. Penguins flap their wings as they swim.
   The South Pole is in Antarctica.
   Thick feathers protect penguins from the cold.
   Seals and whales hunt penguins for food.

122–123

1. Possible questions are:
   (a) Where in the world is the Forbidden City?
   (b) Who was allowed to enter the Forbidden City?
   (c) What are the palaces of the Forbidden City made from?
2. (a) emperor (b) palaces (c) throne

124–125

1. (a) dirty ice (b) warms up (c) long tail (d) centre
2. 2062
3. A comet produces gas and dust called a coma.
   Halley's comet comes around every 76 years.
   Comets are balls of dirty ice.
   A comet's tail can be millions of kilometres long.
   When a comet nears the Sun the nucleus warms up.

126–127

1. (a) bird. Because all the other animals live in the sea.
   (b) sunglasses. Because all the other items are used when it rains.
   (c) chess. Because all the other games need a ball.
   (d) cabbage. Because all the other items are kinds of fruit.
2. (a) clean (b) crown (c) live (d) mouth

128–129

1. (a) S (b) D (c) S
2. (a) rulers in ancient Egypt (b) a sleigh
   (c) because robbers often broke into tombs
3. A pharaoh could be buried in a pyramid.

130–131

1. (a) D (b) A (c) A (d) A (e) A (f) D
2. (a) dark green (b) yellow (c) white
   (d) light green (e) brown
3. lizard

68–69

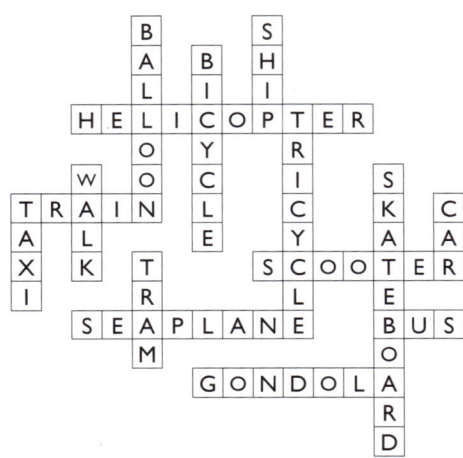

76–77

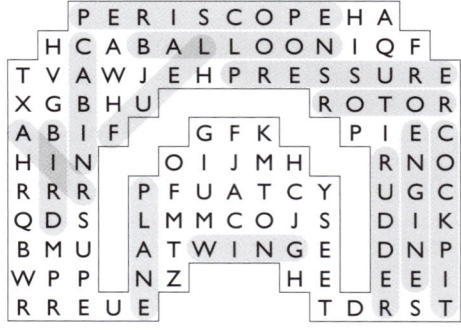

84–85

88–89

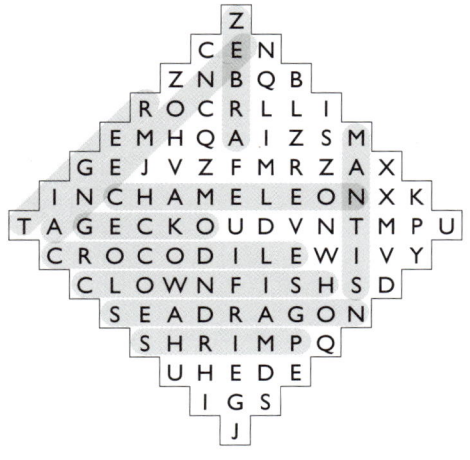

108–109

O	A	E	R	N	L	V	D
N	L	V	D	O	E	R	A
E	N	D	V	L	R	A	O
A	O	R	L	V	D	E	N
V	R	L	N	D	A	O	E
D	E	A	O	R	V	N	L
R	D	N	A	E	O	L	V
L	V	O	E	A	N	D	R

90–91

w	i	n	d
w	a	n	d
l	a	n	d

112–113

1. COFFINS
2. PAINTED
3. MUMMIES
4. CEMETERIES
5. SHEETS

96–97

1. SEA
2. CHOKES
3. OIL
4. DAMAGE
5. SUBSTANCES
6. BEAUTY

114–115

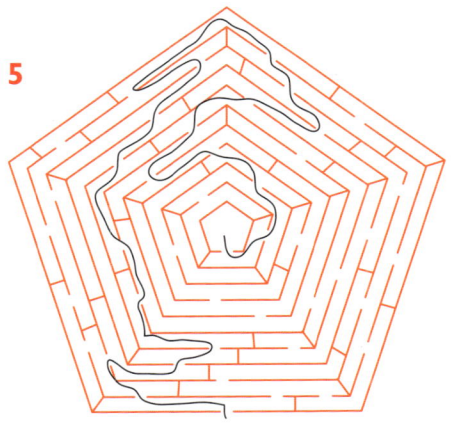

104–105

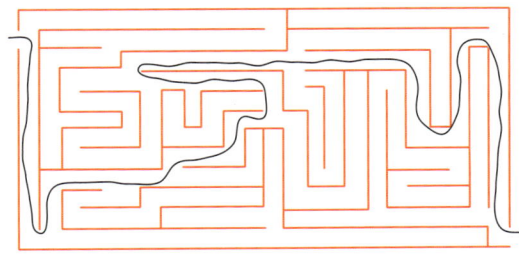

This edition published in 2011
by Australian Geographic
An imprint of ACP Magazines Ltd
54 Park Street, Sydney, NSW 2000
Telephone (02) 9263 9813, Fax (02) 9216 3731
Email editorial@ausgeo.com.au

Australian Geographic customer service
1300 555 176 (local call rate within Australia)
+61 2 8667 5295 from overseas

Conceived and produced by
Weldon Owen Pty Ltd
42–44 Victoria Street, McMahons Point
Sydney NSW 2060, Australia

Copyright © 2009 Weldon Owen Pty Ltd

WELDON OWEN PTY LTD
Managing Director Kay Scarlett
Publisher Corinne Roberts
Creative Director Sue Burk
Senior Vice President, International Sales Stuart Laurence
Sales Manager, North America Ellen Towell
Administration Manager, International Sales Kristine Ravn

Managing Editor Averil Moffat
Concept Design Kathryn Morgan
Designer Juliana Titin
Design Assistant Oliver Black
Images Manager Trucie Henderson
Production Director Todd Rechner
Production and Prepress Controller Mike Crowton

All rights reserved. No part of this publication may be reproduced, stored in a retrieval system or transmitted in any form or by any means, electronic, mechanical, photocopying, recording, or otherwise, without the permission of the copyright holder and publisher.

ISBN: 978-1-7424-5294-4

Printed and bound in China by 1010 Printing Int Ltd

A WELDON OWEN PRODUCTION

Illustration and Photo Credits
4–5 David Kirshner, 7 Stephen Seymour, 9 Iain McKellar, 11 Nicola Oram, 13 Mark Stewart/The Art Agency, 15 Richard Bonson/The Art Agency, 17 Lloyd Foye, 19 Shutterstock, 21 Steven Noon, 22 Tim Hayward, 23tl Guy Troughton, 23tr Tim Hayward, 25 Lynette Cook, 27 Tom Connell/The Art Agency, 28 Simone End, 29 David Kirshner, 31 Christer Eriksson, 33 Richard Hook, 35 James McKinnon, 37 Mark Garlick, 38 David Kirshner, 39 Andrew Beckett, 41 Peter Scott/The Art Agency, 42 Rod Westblade, 43 Rod Westblade, 44 and 45 David Kirshner, 47 Roger Swainston, 49t Peter Bull Art Studio, 49br Digital Stock, 51 Stephen Seymour, 52–53 Ray Grinaway, 55 Christa Hook, 57bl John Mac, 57br Frank Knight, 59 Simon Williams, 61 Peter Schouten, 63 Peter Bull Art Studio, 65 Peter Bull Art Studio, 67 Iain McKellar, 69 and 71 Christer Eriksson, 73 Peter Bull Art Studio, 74 iStock, 75 Iain McKellar, 77c Langdon G. Hells, 77b Alex Lavroff, 79 James McKinnon, 80 Rod Westblade, 81 Trevor Ruth, 82 Mike Gorman, 83 Iain McKellar, 85 Rod Westblade, 87 Chris Forsey, 89 Kim Thompson/Kingpin, 91t PhotoDisc, 91c Mick Posen/The Art Agency, 93 Steve Hobbs, 95 Christer Eriksson, 96 The Art Agency, 97 Corel Corp., 99 Peter Bull Art Studio, 100 Ray Grinaway, 101 Robin Carter/The Art Agency, 103 Peter Bull Art Studio, 105 Tom Connell/The Art Agency, 106bl Susanne Addario, 106br Michael Saunders, 107 and 109 John Richards, 110 Gino Hasler, 111 Luis Rey/The Art Agency, 112 Australian Picture Library, 113 Iain McKellar, 114–115 Ann Bowman, 116 Paul Bachem, 117 Sharif Taraby, 118–119 Gillian Jenkins, 121 Christer Eriksson, 122 Ray Grinaway, 123 Peter Mennim, 125 Lynnette Cook, 126 Simone End, 127bl Ian Jackson, 127br Shutterstock, 129 Richard Hook, 130 Robert Hynes, 131 Colin Newman